*Indians of the Oaks*

# Indians of the Oaks

*By*

MELICENT HUMASON LEE

[SHAH-TĪ', "TALL CEDAR"]

*Founder-Director, Indian Arts League, San Diego, California*

ILLUSTRATIONS BY LESLIE W. LEE

San Diego Museum of Man
1989

Second Reprint Edition
Lithographed in the United States of America

ISBN No. 0-937808-50-4


Originally published 1937 by
Ginn and Company, Boston

First reprint edition 1978 by
Acoma Books, Ramona, California,
for the San Diego Museum of Man

Introduction by Ruth Gautereaux, 1978,
revised by Ken Hedges, 1989

▶ ▶ ▶     ◀ ◀ ◀

*To*

ROSA (WAHSS) AND SANTOS,

CONCEPCIÓN AND DAN,

CARLOTA, CANDELITA, LORENZO,

AND ALL MY OTHER DEAR INDIAN FRIENDS

WHO HAVE GIVEN ME THE THREADS

TO WEAVE THIS LITTLE BOOK

# INDIANS OF THE OAKS

## INTRODUCTION

Welcome to the world of the Kumeyaay—the Indians of the Oaks. It is a world that exists no more. The green valleys resplendent with oak groves and the mountain-to-desert paths described herein still exist for those who search them out, but those patterns of life, the daily activities that linked one generation to the other in the stories of Kwee-tahk, Pi-on, and others, are long gone.

The world of the *Indians of the Oaks* is the land of the people the Spanish called Diegueños, the native inhabitants of the coastal plains, mountains, and desert regions of what is now southern California. It was a land that extended from the Pacific Ocean to the Salton Sink and from the San Dieguito River south to Ensenada in what is now Baja California.

This world was divided in two. The people to the north spoke a different dialect of Diegueño than those to the south and are referred to today as Ipai, the word in their language meaning "people." Those to the south can be referred to as Tipai, the word in their dialect with the same meaning, but today they are generally known by their own name, Kumeyaay. With the coming of the Spanish, these people received a name that gave no consideration to their division, one that characterized a foreign religion rather than gave meaning to a native population. The name Diegueño, after mission San Diego established in

vii

their territory, came into common use when speaking of both groups. There is evidence that in ancient times the name Kumeyaay was used in the northern dialect area as well, and today Kumeyaay is commonly used to refer to all of the people formerly known as Diegueños.

The Kumeyaay lived in groups or bands of about fifteen to thirty people, with larger aggregates occurring when seasonal foods were plentiful or in favored locales such coastal bays and lagoons. Each band belonged to a larger clan or lineage which hunted game and gathered wild foods in a territory that it recognized as its own. For nearly two millennia these people lived in relative peace in their own hills and valleys. They developed the use of acorns as a food, grinding them to a meal with stone tools and learning to leach away the bitter tannic acid. They utilized agave, mesquite beans, cactus fruits, and unnumbered other fruits, seeds, and roots. For the most part, they merely gathered wild plants, but there is increasing evidence that they also transplanted plants or their seeds to better locations either for growing or for ease of harvesting. Plant resources were managed by fire, and seed was broadcast to provide food crops where desired. The practice of agriculture seems limited to those people who inhabited the territory along the New and Alamo rivers in the Imperial Valley. These people had learned to grow corn, beans, and squash in cultivated plots watered by the flood waters of the rivers.

Usually the women did the gathering of wild plants with the men assisting them in the more difficult harvesting. The men hunted large game animals such as deer or bighorn sheep as well as rabbits, or trapped small rodents, birds, and reptiles as a supplement to their diet. In order to take advantage of ripening crops or a concentration of animals, the people moved with the seasons between one or two permanent villages and numerous camp sites.

They did not live in isolation. Contact with other groups for trade or marriage was important. Baskets, pottery, shell for jewelry, stone for tools, and foodstuffs changed hands during these meetings at some favored spot. Dances, games, and other socializing took place as they had for countless generations until the day the Spanish arrived.

Beginning in 1769 with the establishment of the Mission of San Diego de Alcalá by Father Serra, the traditional way of life started to change. At first the coastal Kumeyaay, with whom the Spanish made initial contact, acted peaceably. But as more and more unreasonable demands were made of them and the old ways were threatened, Kumeyaay resentment of the intruders increased. The Spanish were interested in Indians only to convert them to Catholicism and to use Kumeyaay labor to help build the mission system. The Kumeyaay were used to freedom, but the Spanish expected them to remain under their control at the missions. The Indians had never worried about time, but the Spanish regulated their activities with bells.

Within the decade, some of the Kumeyaay rebelled and attacked the mission, but the attack was poorly organized for they had little experience in such matters, and the revolt failed to remove the Spanish. Rather than submit to the difficult new way of life, many of the Kumeyaay moved away from the coastal areas and into the mountains.

In 1821, Mexico overthrew the Spanish government and seized all of the mission lands and the power that they represented. The Kumeyaay who had been missionized fled into "town" and were promptly debased or enslaved. The Indians who were living in the more remote areas found themselves being ousted from more and more of their territory as the outsiders moved onto the land and drove them ever farther into marginal lands.

By the time the Americans took over California in 1848, the traditional Indian culture had been irreparably disrupted. Many of the American immigrants became ranchers and used huge tracts of land, often employing the Indians as ranch hands. This activity introduced rudimentary wage economy to the Kumeyaay. Then, when gold was discovered in the mountains in 1870, American miners and settlers poured into the region, dealing the final blow to the way of life the Kumeyaay had known for two millennia.

Historically, it is not known how many Kumeyaay lived in the area at the time of the Spanish arrival, but modern estimates place the number close to 20,000. Today there are approximately three thousand. Many of these live on reservations, of which there are fourteen in San Diego County, and in Indian communities in Baja

California. Others prefer to live in the cities, filling a wide variety of jobs, and some owning their own businesses. Some maintain close ties with the reservations while others do not. Within the last few years, there has been a strong resurgence of interest and pride in the old ways. It was for the Kumeyaay of today as much as for the non-Kumeyaay reader that Melicent Humason Lee intended *Indians of the Oaks.*

Melicent Humason was an easterner, born in New London, Connecticut, in 1890. She was married there to artist Leslie W. Lee. Shortly thereafter, the Lees moved to San Diego, where they maintained a residence in town and another at a remote ranch in Dehesa, thirty-five miles from the city.

It was the Dehesa property, which the Lees named Hollow of the Hills Ranch, that first brought Melicent Lee into contact with the Kumeyaay. The ranch was situated in an area which had once been intensively occupied by these people and remnants of the population remained there, clinging to the vestiges of their culture while trying to cope with the new. Intrigued by these people and perhaps sensing the impending loss of their culture, Melicent Lee began to spend more and more time with them. Her friends in San Diego commented on her progressively fewer visits to the city, remarking that she showed a preference for the "quiet life of retirement." It was hardly that! A great part of her time was spent with the Indians, traveling with them and participating in their work as they moved from one seasonal site to another, trying to hold to the surviving traces of their traditional ways.

Sometimes Leslie Lee accompanied his wife in this activity, making an occasional painting, but usually she went alone with her Kumeyaay friends. As a sign of their acceptance and esteem, they bestowed upon her a native name.

Melicent Lee took great interest in drawing out the ways of the past from those individuals who remembered them. On one occasion, at her request, two Indian friends constructed a house in the traditional Kumeyaay style. She faithfully recorded the materials and methods of construction used in building the house and later reported on them in an article entitled "The Ancient House of the San Dieguéño Indian," which appeared in *Art and Archaeology* in 1928.

On another occasion, during the same year, the school children of San Diego were invited by the San Diego Museum, now the Museum of Man, to come to Balboa Park for a demonstration and taste of Kumeyaay cooking. The event was arranged by Melicent Lee and two of her Kumeyaay friends who prepared acorn meal and rabbit to show the young people how this was done.

For the 160th anniversary of San Diego's founding she created a Kumeyaay rancheria at the historic San Diego Presidio site. Authentic houses were built and furnished with tools borrowed from the Indians, the San Diego Museum, and various private collectors. Kumeyaay participants were dressed in authentic old-style dress and engaged in traditional pursuits—seed grinding, rabbitskin blanket weaving, basketry, and pottery making. Mrs. Lee hoped that this program would provide the public with a more accurate picture of what Kumeyaay culture had once been like.

However, her interest in the Kumeyaay was not limited to the ways that were gone. She was also concerned with helping her Indian friends achieve the artistic recognition she felt was due them. For this purpose, she presented a lecture at the San Diego Museum entitled "The Indian Speaks for Himself," in which she discussed Indian aesthetics in painting, basket weaving, pottery making, and dancing. She then organized and directed the San Diego Indian Arts League to introduce Indian artists and craftspeople into the community and to educate the public about Indian art.

The culminating effort of her activities was *Indians of the Oaks*—in essence two stories of Indian life in the long ago of San Diego County. Interwoven with the doings of Kwee-tahk, the Herb Woman and baby Wahss, Op-a-chuk, and others are the Kumeyaay tales, games, songs, recipes, and vocabulary gathered by Melicent Lee over the years. Not only is the book a fine adventure story, it is an extremely valuable source of ethnographic materials for Native Americans, students of Indian culture, anthropologists, and historians as well.

The descriptive accounts of Kumeyaay agave gathering, rattlesnake hunting, cradleboard manufacture, bow and arrow construction and use, herb gathering, and other activities that appear in *Indians of the Oaks* are to be found in almost no other publication. Thanks to the dedication of

## Introduction

Melicent Lee, vital information about an important and valued culture that might otherwise have been lost was saved.

So welcome to a world of long-ago. The characters are fictional, drawn from the mind of the author, but the patterns of the characters' lives are real, an accounting of authentic lifeways recorded for us all by Melicent Lee.

Ruth Gautereaux
Former Education Coordinator
San Diego Museum of Man

▶▶▶ ◀◀◀

# Foreword to Teachers

THE SCENES in this book are set about seventy-five years ago, in the foothills of Southern California, where the Kum-me-is lived, and in the desert and mountains where they often journeyed. Similar conditions existed throughout the entire Pacific coast, extending into Arizona, New Mexico, and Lower California.

I spent many years with the Kum-me-i Indians gathering their folklore, their knowledge of nuts, roots, and herbs, and their ancient customs. Most of these old customs are disappearing swiftly in the new life which the Indian lives today. Many customs had almost vanished at that time, but there was always some older Indian who could remember them and enact them for me. It was an old Indian woman who gave me my Indian name *Shah-ti*.

On mountain trails, in desert solitudes, by campfires in lonely places, I gleaned their lore from them. I hunted with them for ollas which their ancestors had hidden in caves; I watched the women gather and prepare acorns and piñon nuts in the forests; I helped them to collect seeds and parch them.

I discovered two old Indian men who could build an ancient house, and I worked with them, flapping the wide leaves of the *Yucca Mohavensis* over the fire to soften them for string, and helping to fetch deerweed for thatch.

Bit by bit I gathered material from real Indian sources, and not once did I use second-hand material. Indeed, I doubt if I could have found much of it in printed form.

MELICENT HUMASON LEE

# A Note on the Pronunciation of the Indian Names

So FAR as possible the Indian names appearing in this story have been spelled to show how they are pronounced. Each word is, however, pronounced in a footnote on the page on which it first occurs. At the end of the book there is also a "Little Dictionary" of the Indian names that occur in the text. The reader may find this useful for later reference, but it is hoped that by providing the pronunciations on the same page as the first occurrences the reading will be less interrupted.

It would be well for the teacher to familiarize herself with the key which has been used in making these Indian names. She will then be able to assist the pupils in pronouncing the words. Before long the children will immensely enjoy adding a few Indian words to their vocabularies, especially since some of them are particularly descriptive.

## KEY

ă *as in* can
ā *as in* cane
ĕ *as in* bet
ē *as in* be
h' *as in* huh
ĭ *as in* hid
ī *as in* hide
kw' *as in* kwuh
n' *as in* nuh
ōō *as in* food
ō *as in* note

ŏ *as in* not
ow *as in* how
oi *as in* oil
ŭ *as in* us
ū *as in* use
tl (to pronounce *tl*, place the tongue at the roof of the mouth in position to say *t* and then let out the breath at either side of the tongue.)

▶▶▶ ◀◀◀

# Contents

## Indians of the Oaks

## Secrets of the Trail

# Contents

# Indians

# of the

# Oaks

▸ 1 ◂

# How I Happened to Live
# with the Indians

I WOKE up and found myself lying in a little hut.
The inside was dark. I crawled to the doorway. It
was a small opening with a curved, or arched, top.
I looked about me. I saw a green valley with dark
mountains all around it.

Many Indians were scattered about the valley.
They were carrying baskets or jars upon their heads
and walking up and down the trails to their little
houses.

One Indian stood close by the doorway of the hut
in which I lay. He was talking to somebody I could
not see. He used a Spanish word once in a while
that I could understand because my grandmother
was Spanish. Many Spaniards lived in California
when it belonged to Mexico, and the Indians learned
Spanish from them.

Through all the chatter I understood the Indian
to say, "When the day grows warmer, we will take
him into the sunlight and feed him."

[3]

"We will . . . feed him!" Then I began to know that I was very hungry and was aching all over. I felt of my bones, but they were all in place.

I was cold. It seemed as if I couldn't wait to be taken into the sunlight. I looked all around me. I was lying on a rabbitskin blanket. It was woven of strips of warm rabbitskins.

Near my head was a big stone with a deep hole in it. Sticking out of the hole was a long, smooth rock.

 These two pieces were a mortar and pestle,[1] used for grinding acorns. I knew what they were because a set of them had stood in our garden for a long time.

Baskets were turned upside down on the earth floor of the hut. A little baby cradle hung from a branch. The sun began to creep in through the arched doorway.

Someone was coming. An old woman crawled through the low doorway. Her face was very much wrinkled. Her chin looked blue where color had been pricked, or tattooed, into the skin. All she wore was two aprons, or skirts, of soft bark. The skirt in back was longer than the skirt in front.

[1] pĕs'l.

[ 4 ]

"*K'yu!*"[1] she called. How was I to know that *k'yu* meant "come"? But I learned to say that word very soon. It was the word I heard most.

I was not afraid. My father had taught me to be brave. The old woman half carried, half dragged me through the doorway. The sun hurt my eyes. I lay on the ground near the hut.

The Indians put down their baskets and jars and gathered around me. They were silent for a long time, then one of them said in my language — the

[1] k'yū'.

[5]

English language of my father and mother: "You have been hurt, but you are better. You rolled off a cliff into our village." He pointed to a high pile of rocks at the edge of the valley. "You have been lying still for many hours. Our medicine man sucked the bad sickness out of you. Now you are well."

I opened my eyes wide and looked at the Indians. The men were naked except for a breechcloth — a narrow strip of deerskin around the hips. They had strong chests and shoulders. Their hair was long and fell in a fringe over their eyes. Their faces were painted with red, yellow, and white paint. Their eyebrows were very thick.

The young women looked like parrots, their faces were so bright with paint. They had triangles and circles and lines and dots of scarlet. Some of them had white rings around their legs.

A few of the old men had rabbitskin jackets covering their chests, and the women had baby cradles hanging on their backs. The babies looked like little chipmunks, with scarlet triangles on their cheeks.

The Indians did not look unkind. Their eyes were merry, and it is the eyes that count. The man who spoke to me was the kindest looking of them all.

"Whom did I leave behind me?" I asked this kind Indian. This was the first thing which came to my mind when he told me that I had fallen. I could remember nothing.

[6]

## How I Happened to Live with the Indians

"That is the queer thing," answered the Indian. "No one could we find. We hunted all the time you lay there quiet." He pointed toward the hut.

I let my mind go back a long way. My mind traveled backward instead of forward. And then I said: "I remember. I left no one behind me. I was alone. My mother and my father are both dead, and a neighbor sent me to live on a ranch. The rancher was not good to me, and I ran away. I ran for two days. I was hungry. I guess I grew dizzy and fell."

The Indians looked at one another. The kind man who spoke English translated my words to the others. An old Indian who had white hair and a ring of abalone¹ shell in his nose spoke in low tones. Everybody listened.

Then the kind Indian said, "The chief says that you may stay with us as long as you like."

I did not know whether to be glad or sorry. And then I thought of the words my father used to say to me, "Experience is good, my son, whether it is pleasant or unpleasant."

I was only ten years old now, but my father had always spoken to me as if I were a man. He had died about a year before.

"Experience is good . . ." I will not run away, I thought.

¹ ăb a lō 'nē.

# ⟩ 2 ⟨

# *The Rattlesnake Hunt*

I HAD lived in the Indian village for a month. I had taken off my ragged shirt and trousers and ran about naked like the Indian boys. My hair was growing long, and I tied it away from my eyes with a cord of mescal[1] fiber, the Indian's string. Mescal is a plant with long, thick leaves from which string is made.

I always carried a bow and arrows with me. Like the other boys, I thought always of hunting, because without food we should die.

One day I was carrying my little bow and arrows down a sweet-smelling trail. Gold and silver ferns grew at my feet. Suddenly I heard the sound of voices above me, and, looking up, I saw three of the young girls of the village in a cave. They were sitting on a flat rock which formed the floor. Their black hair fell all over their shoulders. They looked like three crows.

One of the girls was painting the face of another with a piece of yellow clay, and the third girl was

[1] měs kahl'.

[ 8 ]

grinding seeds with a small round stone in a shallow place in the rock.

After the face-painting job was done, the girl took clay and began to draw curious shapes on the low ceiling of the cave. From where I was standing I could not see what she drew.

Suddenly one of the girls screamed, and they all jumped off the rock and ran away. I climbed up through the small bushes and other brush to the place where they had been. I saw a big rattlesnake crawling from a dark corner of the cave into the sunny spot where they had been sitting.

And then I looked farther in, and I saw a whole nest of rattlesnakes wriggling toward the sunlight. I ran back to the village as fast as I could and shouted: "The rattlers! the rattlers!"

I had heard the Indians talk many times about the spring rattlesnake hunt. I had looked forward to the time when the warm weather would bring the snakes out of their hiding places.

The young men grabbed long, heavy sticks and dashed out all together. An old woman ran her tongue over her lips and said, "We will get the water boiling."

I understood what she said. I was learning the Indian language very quickly. The Indians would say a word to me over and over again. They meant to have me speaking their language very soon.

But how lonely I should have been if Pi-on,[1] the kind Indian who had first talked to me, had not spoken English! An old miner had taught him many English words. English, Spanish, and Indian! These three languages would help me all my life.

We almost ran up the trail. My! those Indians could go fast when they wished! Some of them had pushed their feet into their fiber sandals, so that they  should not slip on the rocks. They said that the thick soles also protected their feet from the snakes. When we reached the opening of the cave, Pi-on said to me: "Do exactly what the rest do. Creep up the sides of the rock. Surprise the rattlers. Pound their heads until they are killed. Go!"

We crept up the rock. A lot of snakes were lying in the sunlight. We struck their heads and killed them by the dozen. Then we tied them by the necks and strung them to a long pole which two of the Indians carried over their shoulders.

Some of the others put their snakes in nets of mescal. I tied mine to a little pole and proudly hung it over my shoulder. I killed only one, but many of the Indians killed several.

The old women were waiting at home, boiling the water in big cooking-jars, or ollas,[2] and stirring the

[1] pī ōn'.          [2] oh'yas.

fire. They coiled up the snakes, without cutting off the heads, and tossed them into the ollas. I started to toss mine into an olla too, but an old woman cried to me just in time: "Save me that one for medicine. I need the oil for my rheumatism." She rubbed her knees with the palms of her hands to show me how lame they were.

And so my snake was saved for medicine.

The other snakes were good to eat, but they smelled pretty bad while they were cooking. But the Indians didn't mind that!

## ▸ 3 ◂

## *Roasting the Mescal*

ONE DAY the chief called his men together and said: "It is time for some of you to go into the desert to get the mescal stalks. The thickest parts are sweet and good, and the old people are hungry for them. And perhaps you can find some yucca[1] stalks on the way. (These yucca stalks were nice to eat.) Bring home everything good that you can find."

"Who shall go?" asked Pi-on, who was the chief's son.

"The young shall go," answered the chief. "It is a long way into the desert for the old. They shall stay here. But you can take your wives."

We prepared for the trip. We were always happy when we were sent on a journey. The women packed their household utensils in carrying-nets. They took cooking-ollas, and little water jars in the mouths of which they stuffed corks of brush.

Op-a-chuck,[2] Pi-on's big, strong wife, carried her favorite little stone metate[3] for grinding seeds. The metate was a large oblong stone, almost flat.

[1] yŭk′a.　　[2] ōp a chŭk′.　　[3] mā tah′tā.

## Roasting the Mescal

The center of the top was scooped out a little. The seeds would be poured into this shallow place and ground with a rubbing stone. The rubbing stone

which belonged to the metate was a flat round stone that fitted the hand.

I had learned to love Pi-on and Op-a-chuck as if they were my own people. They were strong and kind, and I knew that I could trust them.

The women put their basket caps on their heads to protect their foreheads from the cords of the carrying-nets. The men carried their bows and arrows, and nets full of deer meat. They fastened these nets to the fiber belts which they always wore round their waists.

When we reached the desert, Pi-on said: "The women and children will camp here. The rest of us will separate. We must not let one another see what we are doing. If one of us sees another roasting mescal, the mescal will not be sweet."

I felt heavy-hearted. I didn't want to stay with the women and children, and I didn't want to gather my mescal alone. Besides, I didn't know how. I had thought that I was going to stay with Pi-on.

As Pi-on walked away he looked back at me and saw the disappointed expression on my face. He said with a smile: "You are white. You come

under a different law. You will not make the mescal
bitter. And you are not a little child to stay with
women and children. Come with me."

Happy again, I followed Pi-on. I looked back at
the women. They were chattering like blackbirds.
They were sitting under the bushes and kindling
their fires with lighted punk which they had carried
down the mountain in little ollas.

None of their men said "Good-by" to them.
The Indians never said "Good-by." They walked
silently off whenever they were ready to go.

Soon we came to the mescal plants growing out
of the rocky hillside in round bunches. The leaves
were as sharp as daggers. The plants looked like
the century plants that had grown in my mother's
garden. Some of the stalks were covered with
yellow flowers.

"Pi-on!" I cried. "How are we going to dig
out the thick stalks? We have nothing to dig
them with."

Pi-on looked at me sorrowfully. "Have I not
always prepared everything?" he answered.

I felt ashamed. I should have known by this
time that Indians do not forget things which
are important.

Pi-on took a little-worn trail to a cave. I followed
him. We crept into the cave on our hands and
knees.

## Roasting the Mescal

"I do not see anything here," I said, disappointed. Then I could have choked myself. I was doubting Pi-on again. He said nothing. I feared he would send me away if I did not behave more like an Indian.

He took his bow and began turning over the sticks of a wood rat's nest. Pretty soon he uncovered a long, heavy wooden crowbar.

"Here is one," he said. "There should be two. Help me to find the other." I knelt down near the nest and pulled away the sticks with my hands.

"Why doesn't the rat come out?" I asked.

Pi-on laughed. "Do you think this is really a rat's nest?" he asked. "I am the rat. I made this nest to fool people. Many other things are hidden here, too. I have made a deep nest."

"Who would steal your things, Pi-on?" I asked.

"I cannot tell you because you are a white boy," he answered quietly.

I felt hot all over. White people would steal his things, then!

"Don't you ever trust white people?" I asked.

"I trust you," he said.

"I trust you!" I think I was the happiest boy in the world at that moment. My heart sang. I made up my mind right then that the Indians could put their trust in me as long as I lived. If Pi-on had not been an Indian, I should have hugged him, but I knew that he would think hugging very silly.

We both dug away at the mound of sticks. Pretty soon we uncovered another crowbar, then a wooden shovel, then a large olla with the mouth stuffed with leaves, and lastly a very old bow with a bowstring of milkweed fiber.

Pi-on lifted the leaves out of the olla, put in his hand, and pulled out a thin flat circle that shone as he held it up. There was a little hole drilled near one edge. I could see that it was abalone shell.

"They are all like this," he said. "My grandfather drilled these holes. A coast Indian traded these shells to him for some acorns."

He carefully put the shell back into the olla.

"Now we will go," he said. "We shall work near the cave, so the things will be safe as they are."

We walked toward the groups of mescal plants.

"Circle round them," said Pi-on, "and we will choose the best."

We marked each good one with our eyes, and then we began to dig. Each of us used one of the wooden crowbars. We pushed it deep under the fleshy part of the stalk, standing away from the sharply pointed leaves.

After a long time our nets were filled with chunks

of mescal. Then Pi-on said: "I will dig a deep pit at the foot of this slope. Make fire for me!" And he started to dig the pit with his wooden shovel.

Make fire! I had never used the fire sticks before. Pi-on had not even looked at me when he tossed me the sticks. He had been out of matches for several months, because he felt too shy to go to a white man's store.

I put one stick on a flat rock and fitted the rounded end of the other stick into one of the pits, of which there were three in a row. Then I twirled

it between the palms of my hands. I twirled and twirled. My long hair fell over my eyes, my palms ached, but I twirled and twirled.

Pretty soon I sighed loudly. And then I heard a laugh, and I looked up and saw Pi-on looking down at me kindly.

"You will make a good Indian some day," he said. "You have patience. One can never become a good Indian without patience. Now you deserve an Indian name. I will call you *Kwee-tahk*.[1] That means 'Little Man.'"

Kwee-tahk! Kwee-tahk! May nothing ever happen to cause me to lose that name, I thought. I would try to be worthy of it always.

Pi-on knelt down, took the stick out of my red and aching palms, and, with a few very hard twirls,

[1] kwē tahk'.

started a fire. He lighted a bunch of sticks and carried it to the pit.

Pi-on had dug a deep pit. He had lined it with rocks and filled it with dry sweet-smelling sage. Now he made a big fire in the pit. He let the fire die down, and then he took out a few of the hot stones.

He laid the mescal in the pit and put these hot stones over it, so that there were hot stones above and below. He covered the hot stones with brush, then with earth, and he made another fire over the earth.

"Now we will leave it," said Pi-on. "We will forget it and let it cook."

He gathered up the crowbar and the shovel and started to go.

"Are you sure that no one saw us digging or roasting?" he asked.

I ran to a little round hill. I looked all about.

"I am sure no one saw us," I said. "But I can see someone else. He is roasting his stalks in the farther valley."

"Now you have spoiled his dinner for him," smiled Pi-on. "We will let him eat some of ours."

"How long must we wait for the mescal to roast?" I asked. "Will it be long?"

"It will be longer than a night and a day," said Pi-on. "But I have waited more than one moon for a mountain sheep. They are scarce now. The white people are killing them off." Then he began to hum:

" A-mo m'kwah',
A-mo m'kwah,
Toy-yu'ee
T'wum'ee,
A-mo m'kwah,
A-mo m'kwah."

As Pi-on explained the words, they meant

Mountain sheep with horns,
Mountain sheep with horns,
Coming and going,
Coming and going.

"I can see the picture in my head," I said.

"I can see the picture with my eyes," said Pi-on. I followed his look. Far off on a rocky hill beyond us was a sheep coming and going, coming and going. It was the first mountain sheep I had ever seen.

"Are we going after it?" I asked Pi-on.

"We are too late," said he. At that moment I saw a little band of Indians creeping toward the sheep, along the top of the hill. One Indian was kneeling, ready to draw his bow.

"He eats our mescal; we eat his sheep," said Pi-on, as the sheep suddenly fell and tumbled down the cliff. "That is the grandson of the old man who is roasting his stalks in the valley."

# ›4‹

# A Bath in the Desert

NIGHTTIME CAME upon the desert. Pi-on and I lay together by our fire. We had not brought a rabbit-skin blanket with us.

"We are not old women," Pi-on said.

But the desert was cold at night. Pi-on lay down on one side of the fire, and I on the other.

"Pi-on," I whispered, "my back is cold."

"Turn your back to the fire," he said.

Then — "Pi-on," I said, "my front is cold."

"Turn your front to the fire," he said.

Then — "Pi-on," I said, "my back is cold."

"Do not complain," said Pi-on. "Warm yourself as well as you know how, Kwee-tahk. You will soon go to sleep."

Strangely enough I did go to sleep before long. When I awoke, Pi-on was nowhere to be seen. I finally found him in a little valley. He carried a couple of desert quail in his belt.

"Take your bath while I cook the quail," he said.

Take a bath! Where? In the sand? On the rock? I thought he was only joking.

"How can I take a —" But I never finished that question.

Pi-on was looking at me as if he were ashamed of me. I'd take a bath if I had to walk to the Salton Sea! The "Salton Sea" was a lake in the desert a few miles away. I walked away just as if I knew where to go. And then I felt something damp under my foot. It was Pi-on's wet footprint!

I followed his marks easily through the sand. I was back-tracking him. His footprints led away from a pile of rocks. I saw his marks clearly on the stone. But how could he find water up there?

I scrambled up the pile. I climbed over big rocks. And then I stopped in fear. The tracks led straight up the smooth side of a cliff.

I stared and stared at them. And then I saw tiny cracks in the rock. I started to climb up like a monkey. I reached the top. My heart had almost stopped beating, I was so frightened. I dared not look back.

On top of the rock there was a clear, deep pool of rain water. I remembered now that Pi-on had told me about a little lake in the rock where the mountain sheep came to drink.

I plunged into the little pool of clear water and splashed happily. When I climbed out of the pool, I saw a still figure standing at the edge of the pool. It was Pi-on.

## A Bath in the Desert

He lifted my wet body in his arms and carried me down the side of the cliff. When we reached the bottom, he said: "You are as brave as an Indian. But even though you are brave, I do not want you to risk your life slipping with wet feet. When your toes are like fingers, you can go anywhere."

"But you came down in your wet feet!" I said.

Pi-on laughed. "Even an Indian wouldn't do that," he said. "I made the wet marks with my hand on the rock, and I wet my feet when I reached the sand, so that you could track me. I had my water jar with me."

Good old Pi-on! He led me to the little campfire. The quail were toasted brown. Pi-on and I ate them heartily.

"I wonder what Op-a-chuck is eating for her breakfast," I said.

"Maybe she is eating a big fat lizard," laughed Pi-on. "She likes lizards."

"I like quail better," I cried, licking my fingers.

But how did I know? I had never eaten a desert lizard.

That day Pi-on and I collected mesquite[1] wood for baby cradles. Most of the young women had told us to be sure to get some. Many fine-leaved mesquite trees grew in the desert.

"But they all have cradles for their babies already," I objected.

"Foolish boy!" Pi-on said. "A baby grows, doesn't it? And the baby cradle stays the same. They will be putting their babies into larger cradles soon."

"Why do the women strap their babies so tightly?" I asked.

"So that they will not flop this way and that way," Pi-on answered, waving a quail feather in his hand. "What good is a hunter with a weak and twisted back, like an old cedar tree blown about by the wind? What good is a woman with a weak

[1] měs kēt'.

[ 24 ]

back? What good is she on the trail? What good
is she at grinding the acorns? What good is she at
carrying a basket on her head? What good is an
Indian with a weak and twisted back?"

We found mesquite branches that were strong
and even, and we bent them into hairpin shape
after warming them over a fire until
they were soft. We cut short sticks to
go between, so that the cradles would
look like little ladders when finished,
except for the curve at the top.

"How are we going to tie these
sticks to the sides?" I asked.

"Come with me," answered Pi-on.

He led me to a group of little desert
cedars. He stripped off the bark with
his fingers. It was red and rough.
Then he soaked it awhile in the
cooking-olla.

"Now it is soft and fine for the
cradle," he said, and he tied the
straight little sticks into place and wound the fiber
around them. Only an Indian could have made
such a neat job of it.

"Are you going to fix the cedar pillows too?" I
asked. In the village the cradles that I had seen
had thin pillows of twisted bark that fitted exactly
into the cradles.

Pi-on smiled. "The women know more about those things than I do," he said. "I will take the bark home to them and let them fix the pillows. They usually make their own cradles, but I thought I would make a few myself."

He stuffed the bark, the mesquite wood, and the cradles into the carrying-net.

"Get all the bark you can," he said. "All the women will be wanting it."

I gathered armfuls of the bark. I had never slept in sweet-smelling bark like that. My blanket had been made in a factory.

"I wish I had been born a little Indian," I thought sadly. "I should have lain in sweet bark, and my back would have been straighter."

Pi-on seemed to guess what I was thinking. He always knew my thoughts. He said to me, "Your back is not perfectly straight now, but when you pull yourself up the mountain trail in the fall, it will be straighter.

"And your eyes are not far-seeing yet," he said; "but when you look off the mountaintop day by day, they will grow as strong as our eyes.

"And your legs are not very strong yet," he said; "but when you have walked to the mountaintop, your legs will be strong."

I looked at Pi-on's wonderful body, and I wished that I might grow to be like him. I decided that, whatever else I did with my life, I would have muscles that ran and played with one another.

"K'yu!" said Pi-on. "We will hunt for the yucca that has the long, juicy stalk, not the yucca whose leaves we make into string. I will fill my water jar first." He ran back to the cave, where he had stored his things, and drew out a little water jar with a very small mouth. Then he climbed the rocks to the mountain-sheep pool and came down again without spilling a drop.

"There is no water where we are going," he said. He put the jar in the net, which he first lined with sagebrush in order to stop the holes.

We walked single file among the cactus plants. Pi-on wore his sandals, but I had none. Pretty soon my feet felt so hot and sore that it seemed as if I could go no farther. I had stepped on the thorns of an ugly, snakelike cactus, too. Pi-on walked right along without noticing me. I sat down on a rock and began picking out cactus thorns.

Pi-on looked around. Then he began to laugh.

"There is nothing to laugh at!" I said a little crossly.

He laughed again. "You did not know that the sand would be hot? You did not know that cactus spines were sharp? You did not think? Kwee-tahk! Kwee-tahk!" Then he drew out a little pair of fiber sandals from away down deep in his net.

"Here," he said, handing them to me. "My father, the chief, spent several days making these for you. But until you asked, I did not give. Think of everything you need before you go into the desert."

I took the sandals gratefully and put them on my feet. I promised myself that I would think of everything before my next trip with Pi-on. If I had been alone and unprepared, who knows if I could have gone on at all?

The next time I would lie awake the whole night before, if necessary, and ask myself if I had everything. I knew now that he had made me suffer purposely. Even my own father could not have been wiser.

Soon we came upon a little group of barrel-cactus plants of all sizes. Some of them were taller than I. They looked like big cucumbers set on end, armed with sharp spines. We walked among them in our sandals, each with his bow and arrows in his hands. The sun was hot, and I was very thirsty.

"I want water," I said to Pi-on.

"Do you want water, or do you want something to drink?" he asked.

"I want something to drink," I answered. "I am so thirsty that I cannot go on."

"We will save the water for later," he said. "We will get something else." He stopped, and I stopped

## A Bath in the Desert

too. I looked all about. I could see nothing but the desert and the prickly barrel-cactus plants.

Pi-on walked up to one of the plants, picked up a big stone which was lying near it, and smashed off the top of the "barrel." Then he took a stick and pounded the stuff inside until it was soft and mushy.

"K'yu!" he called. "Make a cup of your hands and drink."

I did as he said, and I tasted a warmish drink which I did not like. I made a face.

"I want water," I said crossly.

Pi-on looked at me a long time. Then he pointed to something in the bushes near my side. It was a heap of bones.

"That man wanted water, too," he said quietly. "But he didn't know that this cactus would have saved his life."

I cupped my hands again and took another drink. "It is not so bad," I said.

"It is better than nothing," said Pi-on. "K'yu!" And we kept on walking across the sand.

# ›5‹

# *A Magic Lunch*

IT WAS almost noon before we found the yucca plants. Long, narrow leaves grew around the thick, juicy stalks, which were just ready to pick. The pink buds had not yet opened.

"Look all about you first," said Pi-on; "then choose the best."

We cut many stalks — enough for everybody in the tribe. Pi-on put his stalks into his net and I put my stalks into mine. One of the old men had made me a very nice net out of milkweed fiber.

"The old people get hungry for yucca in the springtime," said Pi-on. "We will roast a stalk for our supper tonight."

"Our supper! Aren't we going to eat anything for lunch?" I asked.

Pi-on smiled. "I have brought our 'lunch,' as you say, with us."

I could see nothing inside the net that looked like lunch. Pi-on reached down deep and pulled out a deerskin bag about as big as a pig's ear. He flattened it out. In the center were many tiny dark seeds.

"Chia¹ seeds," said Pi-on. "Seeds of a bright-blue flower. Op-a-chuck gathered them in the mountains last fall."

He took a little clay bowl from his net and kindled a small fire with his oak punk, which he carried in the bowl. Then he toasted the seeds over the fire, shaking them all the time so that they would not burn.

When they were brown he spread them in a shallow hole in a rock and ground them into meal with a stone. Then he put the meal into the bowl and poured into it some cool water from the little jar.

He stirred the liquid with his finger, and in a few seconds there was a jelly-like mush in the bowl.

"Taste it!" said Pi-on.

I dipped my finger into the mush and then sucked my finger, and it seemed as if I were sucking the juice of all the desert flowers I had ever known. Then I held the bowl to my lips and half drank and half ate the mush until it was all gone. When I looked up I saw Pi-on laughing at me.

"Did you save any for me?" he asked.

A sick feeling came over me. I had eaten it all!

Pi-on laughed again. "I never eat 'lunch,'" he said. "Haven't you noticed that? Indians never ate more than two meals a day before the white people taught them to eat three."

¹ chē'ah.

## A Magic Lunch

Perhaps an Indian needs to eat only two meals, I thought, but I couldn't live that way yet.

After my chia porridge was all gone I felt very sleepy. I wanted to lie down somewhere and have a nap. There was just one little creosote[1] bush near me. "I will lie under that," I thought. Pi-on picked many of the creosote branches, with their sticky leaves of bright green, and stuffed them into his net.

"What are you going to do with those?" I asked.

"Op-a-chuck's mother has a bad cough," he said. "She will stew these leaves and sniff the steam. And others in the tribe have coughs. This is good medicine. Sometimes we drink it too. It is very bitter."

I knelt down and began to crawl under the creosote bush. I brushed away the little twigs which were on my bed.

[1] krē′ō sōt.

[ 33 ]

"Hi!" yelled Pi-on. "Come back! Watch what you are doing!"

I turned cold all over and crept back quickly. Then I stood up.

"Look!" said Pi-on, pointing to the very place where I had been going. I could see nothing but little twigs.

"Look again!" He took a long stick and pointed at the twigs. Still I could see nothing.

"Look again!" He poked his stick into the twigs, and a small sand-colored rattlesnake crept out of the tangle and began to crawl across the open sand in a queer, sidewise way.

"That is the desert sidewinder," said Pi-on. "Some people call it the 'horned rattlesnake' because it has horns of skin. If it had bitten you, you would have died, because you are too far away from the medicine man. He would suck the poison out of the end of your nose if he were here. Keep your eyes open if you want to be a good Indian."

I had disappointed Pi-on again! But when I looked into his face, it wore the sweetest smile I had ever seen.

"All this comes hard, Kwee-tahk," he said. "Every Indian child has to learn these things. But the one who never forgets them — he is the one who makes the best Indian in the end."

I watched the snake. It traveled slower and

[ 34 ]

slower. After about ten minutes it stopped alto-
gether. It seemed to be dead.

"It is dead," said Pi-on, guessing my thoughts as
usual. "The horned rattlesnake travels at night.
It cannot stand the sun. All day it sleeps under a
bush. A little while in the sun, and it is dead."

I looked very carefully before I lay down under
the bush. I poked around with a stick first. But I
was not afraid. Pi-on squatted down beside me.
He did not sleep.

It was dusk when I woke up. Pi-on was still
there. He was rolling mescal fiber over his thighs
with the palms of his hands, twisting it into cord.

"What are you going to do with that?" I asked
sleepily.

"It is good for many things," he answered. "It
is good for sandals and carrying-nets and hair-
brushes. It is one of our strings."

"Where did you get it?" I asked, for I could see
no mescal.

He patted his net. "I brought some pieces with
me," he said. "I have soaked them for many days.
Now they are ready to twist."

I lay under the bush, wondering if I could ever
know as much as Pi-on knew.

"K'yu!" he said suddenly, looking at the sky.
"It is time to roast our yucca. And I've got a
rabbit too. I shot him while you were asleep."

He showed me a desert rabbit hanging from his belt. "We shall have a good supper," he said.

I followed Pi-on up the trail, rested after my long sleep and hungry for my supper.

For two more days we stayed in the desert. The mescal stalks were roasted by that time. We gathered them up carefully and packed them in our nets. We wore basket caps going home. Our load was so heavy that the cords would cut deeply into our foreheads if they were not protected.

On the way back we met the Indian who killed the mountain sheep. He was carrying part of it over his shoulder. I guess he had given the rest away.

We smiled to ourselves because we knew that his grandfather's mescal stalks were bitter. But we knew that his mountain sheep was sweet.

We met others coming from all directions. They had mescal stalks in their nets, and desert quail and rabbits hanging from their fiber belts. One old Indian had as many as twenty-five rabbits in his net.

"What are you going to do with all those rabbits?" I asked him in the Indian language.

"The medicine man's mother wanted some more rabbits for her rabbitskin blanket," he answered. "Rabbits are getting scarce in the village because many of the old people are making blankets."

All the men were carrying heavy loads. They

## A Magic Lunch

had brought with them the good things of the desert — bark, medicine, mescal leaves for fiber, and many other things, besides the mescal stalks.

We joined the women at the foot of the mountain. They were very merry. They had painted their faces in scarlet and yellow and had tattooed their chins black with cactus needles and partly burned wood.

They gathered up their things when they saw us coming. They had collected a great deal from the desert store too.

The women hung their baby cradles on their backs, the naked little children fell into line, and up the trail we started.

"We shall have a feast when we get home," said Pi-on to them all. Pi-on took the place of the chief when his father was not with us. "Mountain sheep, mescal, and plenty of water from *Hah-kwah-nitl.*"[1]

*Hah* means "water," *nitl* means "black," and *kwah* joins the words together. These words mean "Black Spring," which was the name of our village.

[1] hah kwah nïtl'.

# ‣ 6 ‣

## *Pottery Weather*

THE VILLAGE people were very glad to see us. We made a big feast that night around the fire, and we divided all the things that we had brought from the desert.

The days grew warmer. It was just the right kind of weather for making pottery. If the weather were damp or rainy, the pottery would not dry quickly enough.

Op-a-chuck decided to make some new ollas.

"Go down to the creek," she said to me, "and get me some clay."

I lined my net with leaves, hung it over my shoulder, and started for the creek. I hunted carefully for the right kind of clay. I kept going farther and farther. Finally I found some clay that was smooth and red.

"This is the clay," I said to myself. I gathered a lot of it in my hands and put it into my net. It seemed very fine clay.

When I showed it proudly to Op-a-chuck, she took some of it between the palms of her hands

and swiftly rubbed it into a little cake. Then, smiling kindly at me, she shook her head.

"This is not right," she said. "You will have to dig deeper where there is not quite so much sand."

I went to the creek a second time, and I dug deeply with a stick of wild lilac. Wild lilac is very strong. When I returned again, Op-a-chuck said: "This is still not the right kind of clay. You will have to dig still deeper."

"She is very fussy," I thought, but I said nothing.

## Pottery Weather

I knew that white people were particular, but I had never known that Indians were. It seemed much harder to be an Indian boy than a white boy.

I went to the creek a third time. I walked away down toward the south. As I turned around the bend I saw an old Indian digging with a stick.

"What are you getting?" I asked.

"I am getting clay for my wife," he answered. "This is the best clay in the creek."

"May I have some of it?" I asked.

"Take all you like," he said.

Then I knew that this time I was getting the right clay. I could see where it had been dug out for many years — maybe a hundred years or more. Who knows?

Op-a-chuck rubbed this clay between her fingers. She smiled happily. "You will make a fine Indian some day," she said.

She didn't know that I had met the old man digging clay for his wife. But the next time I should know for myself which clay to get.

In a few days Op-a-chuck started making her ollas. She sat in the sunshine and neatly placed all her things around her. The other women gathered near her with their children.

Op-a-chuck was the best olla-maker in the tribe, and she knew it. She broke off a piece of dry clay, put it on her stone metate, and rubbed it into

powder with a rubbing stone. She felt of the powder
that she had rubbed so carefully with her fingers.

"It is not fine enough yet," she said.

So she put the powder in a
*sah-wil*,[1] or winnowing-tray. This
was a round basket, almost flat,
in which seeds were tossed up so that the wind could
blow away the husks. Now Op-a-chuck was shaking

[1] sah wĭl'.

the basket up and down to bring the lumps of clay to the top. Then she scraped the lumps back onto the metate and ground them again. When the powder was ready, it was as fine as dust.

She mixed it with water which she kept in a little olla by her side, and worked it with her hands into a smooth clay. The children reached out their little fingers to snatch pieces of the clay for tiny ollas. They made funny little jars that did not sit evenly upon the ground.

After the clay was smooth enough to work, Op-a-chuck patted some of it into a large flat cake, which she laid over the base of one of her old ollas so that the bottom of the new olla would be correctly curved.

When the base was just right, she began to make rolls of clay between the palms of her hands. The clay rolled beautifully. It did not fall apart. She added a coil to the olla base and pressed it into shape with her fingers.

Again and again she added coils. When the base was big enough, she took it off the old olla. Then she pressed the coils into shape on the outside with a little wooden paddle and on the inside with a short clay paddle.

As the olla grew into the wide, round shape of a cooking-olla, one of the women said, "I will exchange my seed basket for your olla."

But Op-a-chuck shook her head. "I do not need a seed basket. I can make a seed basket as well as you can."

Everybody laughed at that, because they knew that she was right. There was no household task that Op-a-chuck could not do well.

When the olla was finished, Op-a-chuck said: "Now I will let it dry out. When it is perfectly dry, I will fire it in the pit. It may take two or three days to dry."

She walked toward the pit to see that everything was ready. The pit was lined with stones. Brush for the fire lay beside it.

What a fine figure she had! She might have seemed too large to some white people, but I had learned to like the big, strong, comfortable Indians best. To me they always seemed like mountains in which I could hide when I was cold or tired.

Op-a-chuck's long hair fell to her waist, and her face was painted with scarlet stripes and dots. Around her neck she wore a string of deerskin with a piece of abalone shell hanging from it.

"*Hun!*" [1] (Good!) she said. "Soon we shall be eating *shah-wee* [2] out of my olla." *Shah-wee* means "acorn mush." Op-a-chuck smacked her lips. "When the summer is done we shall gather our acorns," she said. "Now there is much to do to

[1] hŭn.  [2] shah wē′.

[ 44 ]

get ready for the journey. I will start a new seed basket soon."

She smiled to herself. "Seed basket! seed basket! She wants to exchange a seed basket for my olla! Her basket wouldn't hold seeds." Then she gathered up all her materials and walked off to her little hut.

# Op-a-chuck Gives a Basket Party

OP-A-CHUCK'S cooking-olla had been fired, and it hadn't cracked a bit. It stood upside down in her hut, ready for its mountain journey in the fall.

Now she was planning to make a seed basket. The other women were starting baskets of several kinds also, so they all walked down to the creek one morning to gather basket fiber. I walked along too, with my little bow and arrows, as I wanted to hunt some quail for supper.

Where the grass and reeds grew thickest in the dry creek bottom, Op-a-chuck stopped and looked about her.

"Here is the best place," she said. "The *kw'ni*[1] is tall and thick." The kw'ni was used as the basket wrapper, the reed which is wrapped around the inside filler.

Op-a-chuck took one reed in both hands and pulled it out of the creek bottom with all her strength. At its lower end the reed was a golden-brown color which she could weave into a beautiful

[1] kw'nĭ'.

[46]

pattern. The other women pulled the reeds in just
the same way. They all chatted together happily.

Op-a-chuck gathered a great bundle of these long,
willowy reeds. She tied them at both ends with
fiber and then she put the bundle on her head,
holding it with one hand. The other women did
the same. I hunted through the bushes, watching
for a flock of quail, but the women walked in single
file across a meadow.

Soon we came to a marshy spot almost covered with bunches of grass, out of which rose long, feathery stalks.

"Hun! hun-nah!"[1] cried the women all together. "Good! good!" They were glad to find the deer grass, which was used as the basket filler, growing so tall and thick.

"If we had not burned off this basket grass last year," said Op-a-chuck, "the stalks would not be tall and thick now."

That was the first time I had ever heard that the Indians cultivated their basket grass. Fire was their way of cultivating.

It was very pleasant in the clearing. I lay down between the bunches of grass while the women worked. They all gathered the pale-yellow stalks, nipping them off cleanly at the base with their sharp fingernails. With their winglike bark skirts and their merry talk they seemed like a flock of brightly colored, twittering birds.

When they had collected huge bundles of these stalks, they set them on their heads with the reeds and took the trail for home. On the way back I shot three fat quail in the sumac bushes and hung them from the little belt of twisted fiber that I always wore.

"Now we shall have a fine supper," I thought.

[1] hŭn′nah.

## Op-a-chuck Gives a Basket Party

When we reached the village again, Op-a-chuck asked all the women over to her house, so that they could start their baskets together. They laid down their bundles of reeds and deer grass.

One of the women hung her baby cradle on the limb of a tree, close to the trunk. No sooner had she placed it there than there was an angry chirping in the tree. It seems that she had hung her baby in front of a wren's hole, and the mother wren couldn't get into her nest to feed her little ones. The father wren was doing all the scolding. The woman hung her baby on another bough after that.

Op-a-chuck untied her bundle of the green kw'ni, pulled out one of the reeds, held the thick end between her teeth, and split the reed with her fingernails. She split it into four parts. None of the other women could do that. They could split the reed into only two or three parts.

After she had split several reeds she coiled them into a little circle, tied them together in two places, and slipped them into an olla filled with water. This is the way she softened them.

Then she peeled off the husks from the stalks of deer grass and laid the stalks neatly on the ground. Now it took only a few seconds to gather a little fiber into a soft nest and start her basket.

She sharpened her bone awl on a rock. "This awl is getting too short," she said. "When Pi-on kills another deer, I will take out the heel bone and make another awl."

"I have a coyote's rib bone," said one of the other women.

"That is good too," said Op-a-chuck.

The women became silent as they started their baskets. They poked their awls into the tiny nests of fiber and then put a pointed end of the kw'ni into the hole they had made. Then they stuck a

few stalks of deer grass, or filler, into the nest and coiled the reed over it. Thicker and thicker they fed in the deer grass, making the coils larger as the circle grew. Soon the coils would be the size they wished for the rest of the basket. Then they would keep them exactly the same.

This beginning must be made very carefully. The women worked for a long time without speaking. It was hard to go around such a small circle.

They worked all the rest of the day. Only when it was too dark to see did they put their bone awls into the hollows of the baskets they had started, shake their skirts free from the odds and ends of basket grass, and take their own little trails to their homes.

Op-a-chuck and I did not have far to go, because we were sitting right in front of our hut. We crawled inside and roasted the quail for our supper.

# ▸ 8 ◂

## *Deer Sinew and Hawk Feathers*

THE SPRING turned into summer. The men started getting their bows and arrows into shape for the trip up the mountains in the fall. They tightened the strings of their bows and made new arrows.

My willow bow was split, and so I made another. I notched the ends for the bowstring. I made the string out of deer sinew.

Then I went down to the marshes with an Indian boy. We wanted to get some carrizo[1] cane for arrow shafts. The carrizo cane looks like bamboo except that it is smaller.

This boy was the grandson of the medicine man, and I had wanted to play with him for a long time, but he would not play with me. His name was *Hutl-yah-mi-yuck,*[2] which means "Moon in the Sky." He was called by that name because there had been a moon in the sky when he was born.

¹ kah rrē′sō.          ² hŭtl yah mī yŭck′.

## Deer Sinew and Hawk Feathers

We found a nice bunch of cane. We gathered bundles of it and took them home.

Then we followed another trail up the dry hillside to collect chamiso[1] wood for arrow points. The whole hillside was covered with this chamiso, with its tiny, needle-like leaves. The little stone heads, or arrow points, were fastened onto these long wooden points in time of war.

"We had better get all we want now," said Hutl-yah-mi-yuck, "because the men are going to burn over all these hills pretty soon."

"Why?" I asked.

He looked at me without saying anything. Then finally he said: "You are always asking foolish questions, the others say; but that is because you are a white boy. White boys do not look with their eyes nor hear with their ears." And then he explained, "They burn the brush so that many seeds will ripen another season."

He had hurt me more than he knew. I had tried so hard to learn the wisdom of the Indian. Should I always be foolish? Hutl-yah-mi-yuck saw my unhappiness, and he said in a kind tone of voice, "But you never ask the same question twice, they say, the way all the rest do."

"Where did you know 'all the rest'?" I asked.

"In school," he answered. "I went to school

[1] chah mē′sō.

three days. Then I ran away. I couldn't understand the teacher. She was pointing with a stick at a big paper with many colors of paint. She said that the green paint was forest and that the blue paint was water. I know that is not true, because I have seen the forest and I have seen the water, and they are not paint."

He spoke a few words in English, a few words in Spanish, and a few words in Indian. I knew that he was talking about a colored map, but I said nothing.

I had forgotten all about school. Now I longed to get back to my white friends. But Hutl-yah-mi-yuck was speaking again: "We have everything now but the hawk feathers. The little sharp-shinned hawk has been hiding from us."

"Pi-on has some hawk feathers," I said. "And he has plenty of deer sinew."

We tied our chamiso into neat little bundles and started for home.

Then we set to work. I was very proud of my skill. Pi-on had taught me to make arrows, and I could make them as well as the other boys. I put my stone *hup-chutl*,[1] or arrow straightener, into the fire to get it hot. The arrow straightener is a small oval stone with hollows, or grooves, in it.

When the hup-chutl was hot, I chose a straight piece of carrizo cane that had not split and placed

[1] hŭp chŭtl'.

it in the groove of the hup-chutl. Then I straight-
ened it here and there until it was perfect.

I whittled a piece of chamiso into a sharp point
and made the point hard by leaving it in the fire a
few minutes. Then I stuck the other end, which I
had whittled just a little, into the hollow carrizo.

Hutl-yah-mi-yuck was straightening his arrow in
a beautiful hup-chutl which his grandfather had
made. It had three grooves in it, polished from
long use, and it had little
crisscross marks on it.
Mine was plain.

I burned the hawk
feathers until they were the right shape for arrows,
and then I took a piece of deer sinew and tossed
it into my mouth. I chewed it until it was soft.

I fastened the feathers to the shaft with the

sinew and also wrapped the sinew around the end of the carrizo where it joined the point. I didn't want the cane to split. I made several arrows in a short time.

"I am going to try my bow and my new arrows," I said to Hutl-yah-mi-yuck. I looked over at him.

He was already drawing back his bowstring.

I knew right then the difference between the white boy and the Indian. The white boy says, "I am going to do this." The Indian does it. The white boy says, "What is this?" The Indian looks at it and finds out what it is for himself. The white boy asks many silly questions, but the Indian thinks out the answer without asking.

I drew back my arrow and let it fly over the meadow. "Hun!" I said to myself.

"Hun!" said Hutl-yah-mi-yuck. "Our arrows are good." From that moment I liked Hutl-yah-mi-yuck. He did not say, "My arrows are good." He said, "Our arrows are good." He spoke just as if I were an Indian boy, too.

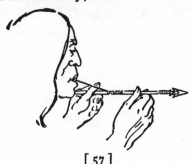

# ⟩ 9 ⟨

# *It Takes Two People to Build*
# *a House*

---

Pɪ-ᴏɴ ᴀɴᴅ Oᴘ-ᴀ-ᴄʜᴜᴄᴋ were talking by the fire in the little hut. "We shall soon be going to the mountains," said Pi-on. "When we come back the rains will fall. Perhaps they will fall before we come back. Our house will not last another winter. We should build a new house before we go."

Op-a-chuck looked unhappy. "I like this house," she said. "Happiness has come to me in this house. Perhaps the new house will not bring me good luck."

"You talk like a foolish woman," said Pi-on. "I will start building the house tomorrow."

Early in the morning he called to me: "K'yu! We have no time to lose. We must start right away."

We went far down the hillside to gather yucca leaves for cord. We cut off the leaves at the base. Then we tied them into bundles, which we carried home in our nets.

## It Takes Two People to Build a House

We made a little fire and held the leaves over the blaze, moving them so that they would not burn. Now the leaves were soft enough to tie together.

Then we chose a place that was better than the old location. It was protected from the west wind by a little hill, and the sun shone in from the south. It was near the creek, where ran the freshest water.

Pi-on walked around in a circle, mapping out the place where the house would stand. When he was satisfied he said, "We will dig the post holes here."

We dug deep holes with crowbars of wild lilac, and then we cut young oak and sycamore trees for the frame. Pi-on had an ax that he had got in trade for a mountain-lion skin at the store before the strange new storekeeper had come to town. In the old days he would have burned the trees at the base instead of cutting them.

The next morning we fastened the poles together at the top with our yucca cord and put other young trees for crossbars round the poles in circles until we had a neat little frame that looked like a bird cage. The small doorway was arched.

"How are we going to cover it?" I asked.

Pi-on pointed toward the hillside. "Do you see the *hee-waht*?" [1] he asked. "You call it 'deer broom.' It is very thick and bushy. It will keep off the rain."

[1] hē waht'.

We gathered great bundles of the hee-waht. It was so lightly rooted that we pulled it up easily. Each of us put a bundle on his back, and as we went down the hill we looked like walking bushes.

"Now we shall need a long needle," said Pi-on. He whittled a needle out of willow. It was a yard  long and had an eye in one end.

We set a pile of hee-waht upright against the frame of the house. Then I crawled inside the house, and Pi-on threaded the needle with the wide yucca thread, poked the needle under a crossbar of the frame, and I un-threaded the needle, pulled it through the thatch, threaded it again, and poked it this time over the crossbar. Then Pi-on tied the two ends together.

In this way we fastened the deer-broom thatch to the house frame. Pi-on said it always took two people to build a house. We had to crawl up the sides to tie the thatch near the top. We laid very heavy brush on the roof.

It took us several days to finish the house. It was very neat and smelled as sweet as ferns. We lighted a fire on the earth floor to make it cozy.

Pi-on was satisfied. "The house is good," he said. "Now we shall all keep dry and warm when the wet season comes."

## It Takes Two People to Build a House

We called all the tribe together to look at our new house. They gathered around it and began to sing:

> "Ee-wah' mo-chow'ah,
> Shah-yu'mee, shah-yu'mee,
> Shah-whur'ee, shah-whur',
> Shah-pi'ee, shah-pi'ee,
> Chu-mee,
> Kwee-yow."

Pi-on told me the meaning of the words and explained that the word *kwee-yow* was so old that even his father couldn't remember the meaning of it. The Indian language had changed since some of the oldest songs were made, he said. In English the song would mean:

> Build the house.
> Tops together,
> Tops together.
> Make a circle,
> Make a circle.
> Slanting, slanting,
> It is held up.

Op-a-chuck did not sing with the rest.

"I like my old house best," she said. "This house will not bring me luck. It feels lonely."

"You make the tribe unhappy when you say that," said Pi-on. "You have the best house in the valley."

Op-a-chuck said nothing, but her eyes looked troubled.

# ‣ 10 ‣

# *Going for Acorns*

THE TIME had come for the trip up the mountain-side to gather acorns. The weather was clear and bright. The evenings were cool.

The men collected their bows and arrows, and the women packed their nets. Everything they needed for the trip they stuffed into them: cooking-ollas, rabbitskin blankets, medicine bark, water jars, and other things.

Op-a-chuck called to me and asked me to get her some seeds of the white sage, which grew freely in a small valley by the hut. "We might use them on the trail," she said; "they make nice mush."

I gathered many branches of the white sage, and Op-a-chuck broke off the seed husks, rubbed them between the palms of her hands to loosen the seeds, and then winnowed the seeds in her winnowing-tray. Soon they were clean and shining. She slipped the seeds into a little deerskin bag and tucked the bag into her net.

We started up the mountain trail single file, the men walking ahead with their bows and arrows in their hands. Some of the men carried heavy loads, too. They wore the same kind of basket caps that the women wore.

Many of the women carried babies on their backs, firmly strapped to the cradles. The little children followed carefully along, their eyes ever on the watch for rattlesnakes. I had learned to walk as the Indian walks — always watching with my eyes and always listening with my ears.

When we were halfway up the mountain we all stopped to drink water at a spring. The water flowed down a little path in a rock. Op-a-chuck filled her water jar with fresh spring water, stuffed a handful of dry leaves into the opening, and carefully set the jar in her net. "I may need some along the way," she said.

The rest of us knelt by a little pool in a rock, where the water was gathering, and drank thirstily.

As I knelt there alone, after the others had walked along, I suddenly noticed a mark in the black mud near the edge of the rock. It was the print of a foot in a heavy boot such as white men wore.

Fear crept over me. It seemed as if that boot were crushing out my happiness. I ran to join the others, where I felt safer.

We spent the night at the end of the trail. After the warm valley below, it was fearfully cold on the mountaintop. The stars were high up and clear,

## Going for Acorns

and the wind ran over our heads. Somehow I felt
sad and lonely as I gathered firewood with the rest.

Op-a-chuck seemed to guess how I felt. "This
is your first trip to the mountain," she said. "The
mountain is not a friend like the valley, but it is
a friend just the same."

I was a little afraid of mountains. It was on this
very mountain trail that I had run away and rolled

down the side of a cliff into the valley below. So it was not my first mountain trip, after all.

The Indians built a fire against a steep rock. Op-a-chuck drew a piece of deer meat out of her net, and others shared rabbits that they had shot on the trail. The old fellow whose mescal was bitter had brought along the leg of a mountain sheep.

Soon the women were busy cooking the dinner, and I helped to keep the fire burning. After we had eaten our dinner we all sat around the fire and sang songs.

The song-maker sang his own song. "This is a woman's song," he said. "I made it only for women." He sang:

> "O-o ch'mee',
> Pahn-yu-a-o-mee',
> Hut-a-pah' ch'mee',
> Pahn-yu-a-o-mee',
> Mah-kwee num-sup',
> N'yah-mi ko-kahch',
> Pahn-yu-a-o-mee'."

The song means

> The owl sings,
> The coyote sings,
> Near my house,
> Early in the morning,
> At daybreak.

## Going for Acorns

As the song-maker began to sing this song over again, the women and children sang with him. And far off, at the edge of the brush, we heard a coyote howl, and away up in a pine tree over our heads an owl hooted, as if he knew that the song was about him.

"Now I will sing a song that my grandfather made up," said the song-maker. "It is a song about a bear in the Cuyamaca[1] Mountain. The Spaniards did not call our mountain by the right name. They said 'Cuyamaca.' Our name is *Kwee-muck*.[2] " (*Kwee* means "cloud," and *muck* means "behind." The cloud, or fog, always lies behind the mountain.)

"Bears do not live here now," said the song-maker (we were right on Kwee-muck then), "because the white people have killed them all."

He shook his rattle made from the shell of a turtle and sang the song about the bear:

> "Nah-mul' ch'wi-yah-wee',
> Hah-mah-nahtl', hah-mah-nahtl',
> Nah-mul' ch'wi-yah-wee,'
> Hah-pah-su'ee, hah-pah-su'ee,
> Nah-mul' ch'wi-yah-wee',
> Hah-mah-natl', hah-mah-natl',
> Nah-mul' ch'wi-yah-wee'."

[1] koo yah mah'kah.
[2] kwē mŭk'.

In English the song means

The bear holds him and blows, *Bur-r!*

The song-maker said: "There is a story that goes before each song. And this is the story that goes before this song. An Indian on Kwee-muck Mountain met a bear, and the bear caught him and blew *Bur-r!* with his angry breath."

I was afraid. I didn't dare look into the dark corners. The children sat in a circle staring at the song-maker. The fire threw strange lights upon their faces. They had heard the story and the song many, many times, but they never tired of it.

The women began to get very sleepy. They lay down in a circle close together. They tried hard to keep awake to hear the songs, but the lullaby of the wind overhead made them drowsy. And they were very tired too. The men were already asleep.

Only the song-maker and I stayed awake. Somehow I could not sleep.

The song-maker laughed. "Now I will sing the 'Sleepy Song,'" he said, "and nobody will answer." And he sang:

> "Sho-mahch mi-ah-cah',
> Sho-mahch mi-ah-cah',
> Mi-ee pah-o-rah',
> Mi-ee mahn-yah-yah',
> Sho-mahch mi-ah-cah'."

## Going for Acorns

When you know the meanings of the words the song will be like this in English:

> Go to sleep where you lie!
> Your eyeballs are sleepy:
> Your eyeballs are shut.
> Go to sleep where you lie!

I heard the song-maker sing this song only once. Maybe he sang it twice. I do not know. For my eyeballs went fast asleep.

# · 11 ·

# *Dancing to Keep Warm*

---

EARLY IN the morning we started in the direction
of the oak woods. We felt rested and strong after
our night of sleep in the open. We had been so
tired that the cold couldn't keep us awake.

Then, too, I was getting so used to cold that I
could lie naked by the fire at night and not even
wish for a blanket. It seemed as if my body were
clothed with fur.

In a little while we came to the sweet-smelling
pines and cedars of the forest. Among these mountain evergreens were scattered huge black-oak trees
which were unlike the live oaks of the lowlands.

The leaves were large and were golden in color at
this time of the year. It was like stopping in the
heart of a fire, to make our camp among the oak trees.

Soon the forest was like a hive of bees which
are suddenly wakened by the sun shining into the
opening of the hive. The men were running down
the slopes to gather brush for shelters. So we were
going to sleep in cozy little houses, after all! I had
wondered what we were to do.

## Dancing to Keep Warm

The women walked over to the oaks and chose the trees which had tossed down the very fattest acorns. All over the ground these fat acorns were lying.

The women took off their basket caps and filled them to the brim. Then they dumped the acorns into huge seed baskets, or into nets which were spread open on the ground and lined with leaves.

## Indians of the Oaks

It was a scene which I never forgot — the Indians, with their long hair, painted faces, and willow-bark skirts, gathering nuts in their brown fingers, and the naked little children running from tree to tree, hunting for the fattest acorns. Sleeping babies were wrapped up in cradles. Little shades of woven bark protected their eyes from the sun.

"Do not pick the wormy acorns," said Op-a-chuck to me, as I busily threw the nuts into a deerskin. "They have tiny holes in them, and they are lighter in color than the others."

I looked over the acorns that I had gathered. Half of them were wormy. "Oh, there is so much for me to learn before I can be like an Indian!" I thought.

It took all day to gather enough acorns for the tribe. The Indians had to make sure that they had enough for another year also, as they never could be sure of the acorn crop.

"There may be no acorns next year," said Op-a-chuck. "We always have to think of one year ahead."

Not until it was dark did we go back to our camp. The men had put up brush shelters for us, and we were as cozy as could be. We cooked our supper in our own little shelter. We ate a fine fat pine squirrel which Pi-on had shot with his bow and arrow. Op-a-chuck cooked it between two hot rocks. My! but it was good!

After our supper Op-a-chuck said: "We are going over to the big fire tonight to crack acorns. Everybody will be there."

I ran over to the big fire. It was blazing in the middle of the clearing. Dozens of women and children were seated around it, all with rounded stones in their hands and other stones on the ground before them. They were all cracking acorns. *Crack, crack, crack!* The sound echoed through the forest.

Hutl-yah-mi-yuck was there, too. I sat down beside him and took one stone and began cracking open an acorn upon a stone before me. I smashed the acorn in pieces.

"You do not crack it right," said Hutl-yah-mi-yuck. "What good is a smashed acorn? Take it this way." He set the point of the acorn in a tiny hole in the rock at his feet, took his round stone, and lightly hit the blunt end of the acorn. This cracked the nut nicely in two.

Then he pulled the shell open with his fingernails, and there were two firm nut meats inside. "Now, these are good for something," he said.

The next time I cracked my acorn better. And the third time I did it perfectly. I didn't even hit the fingers which held the acorn in place.

## Indians of the Oaks

The men did not crack the acorns. They stood in little groups around the fire, sang songs, shivered a little in the cold, and then began to dance to keep warm. I wondered to myself if Indian dancing began by just hopping up and down to keep warm.

The Indian dancers sang as they danced. Their voices carried a long way. They were all strong men. Their black hair swung about their faces. Their bodies were painted in scarlet and yellow and black, and their muscles played with one another, just as I wanted mine to do. I felt of my muscles. They were beginning to dance, too.

The Indian dances were very different from the Spanish and American dances I had seen. They seemed very simple to me at first, just a lifting of one foot and then the lifting of the other foot.

But after a while I could see that there was a great difference between the steps of the dances. They were not so simple, after all.

When I felt quite sure that I should not make a fool of myself, I joined the men and danced in single file with them. They danced many hours, and I kept on dancing, too.

But when I woke up late next morning I couldn't seem to think how I had found my way into my own little corner in the shelter. And then I saw Pi-on laughing at me as he tightened his bowstring near my bed of leaves.

## Dancing to Keep Warm

"You danced yourself to sleep," he said, guessing my thoughts as usual. "You fell down at the end of the line, and I picked you up and put you in your corner."

"But how did you know that I had fallen?" I asked in wonder. "You were the first in the line of dancers."

"And the last meets the first," he said. "If I had not been watching for you in the path, the Indians would have danced right over you. You fell in a dark shadow, Kwee-tahk."

### Indians of the Oaks

Good Pi-on! How long would he be my friend and take care of me? I felt as if I were losing him already. I wanted to throw my arms around his neck, but I knew that he would think it silly. Sometimes I wished that Indians showed their feelings the way white people do.

# ▸ 12 ◂

# *Hutl-yah-mi-yuck and I Weave*
# *a Storage Basket*

---

AFTER I had taken my morning bath in the little pool at the foot of a cedar tree and eaten my breakfast of cold rabbit, I ran into the grove of oaks. All the Indians were as busy as chipmunks. They were spreading their acorn meats on big pieces of bark.

"Why are you doing that?" I asked Op-a-chuck, as she scattered the meats evenly with her brown hands.

"Can't you see with your own eyes?" asked Op-a-chuck, sternly. "Must you be told everything?"

"I can see with my own eyes that you are spreading them out to dry," I said, ashamed of myself. I knew the answer to my question before it was out of my mouth. When should I learn to think before I spoke?

"*Hah*," (Yes) said Op-a-chuck. "You are right. It will take several days for them to dry. With a

stick we will keep turning their sides to the warm
sun. When their little red skins wrinkle up easily
between our fingers, then we shall know that they
are dry. If they are not dry, they will stick to the
stone pestle when we grind them."

"But what shall we do all the time that we are
waiting?" I asked, disappointed. I had hoped that
we were going to grind the meats right away and
that I should soon eat shah-wee.

"We have many things to do," said Op-a-chuck,
wisely. "We have the fruits of the wild rose to
gather, for they are sweet and good, and roots in
the forest to dig, and berries to find. And we have
the big *sho-kwin* [1] to make. That is the most important thing of all."

"What is the big sho-kwin?"

"The big sho-kwin is the storage basket. Every
year we make one sho-kwin or more in the forest.
We store enough acorns in it for another year,
for some years there are no acorns on the trees.
We sometimes make a sho-kwin at home too if we
have enough acorns."

"But Pi-on told me," I said, "that the Indians
stored their acorns in big ollas in the caves near
the village."

"We do that too," said Op-a-chuck. "What do
you think would happen to our acorns if we kept

[1] shō kwĭn'

[ 78 ]

them in the hut? We should make more shah-wee than we could eat.

"We should say: 'Let us have a big feast today. Let us have a big feast tomorrow. We have plenty of acorns —'

"But when the acorns are away up in the caves, and the trail is hard and rocky, do you suppose we are going to run up there often? *Mow!* (No!) We go up there only when it is very necessary. We put the acorns in the cave to protect ourselves against starvation and to hide them from some lazy people that steal." She looked sidewise at a fat woman who was curled up asleep in the sunshine.

"But when do you go and get the acorns in the sho-kwin?" I asked.

"In the spring. All winter long the sho-kwin rests in a tree, in the crotch where the trunk divides into branches. The snow leans its elbows heavily upon it, but it cannot crush it down. All winter it rests in the tree."

"I want to make the sho-kwin now," I said.

"And so do I!" called out a voice, and there was Hutl-yah-mi-yuck coming toward me. "Let's go down to the creek to cut the willows for it, Kwee-tahk."

I ran along with Hutl-yah-mi-yuck. He carried his new bow and arrows in his hand. He had

[ 79 ]

painted his bow with wide rings of red paint. His hair was tied back with a twisted cord of mescal fiber.

He ran down the trail as sure-footed as a coyote. I was getting pretty sure-footed myself, only sometimes I stepped on a pointed pebble that hurt the sole of my foot for days.

Soon we reached the bottom of the slope. It was cool and moist down there. A few willows grew thickly. Hutl-yah-mi-yuck and I began cutting some willow branches.

"Now we have enough," said Hutl-yah-mi-yuck, looking over his shoulder to see how many I had cut. "You have more than I have."

He told me that I had more than he had! I think he really liked me.

"Hutl-yah-mi-yuck," I said, with my voice choking, "if ever I go back to live with the white people again, will you still be my friend?"

Hutl-yah-mi-yuck sat down on a rock and thought very quietly. He held the big bunch of fragrant willows in his arms. Then he said slowly, "If you go back to the white people and still keep kind thoughts of us in your heart, I will be your friend."

Little Hutl-yah-mi-yuck! I shall never forget his strong brown body in the sunlight. I could not say a word. I felt that words would mean nothing.

## *Hutl-yah-mi-yuck and I Weave a Basket*

Only acts would count for anything. And this is what I learned that day: not to promise, but to do! I knew that many white people were kind friends to the Indians always, and I knew that I could be the same.

We walked up the mountain trail, one behind the other, with the bundles of willows on our backs. Pi-on had been right when he said that mountain-climbing would make my muscles strong. They were almost as hard as those of Hutl-yah-mi-yuck. When we reached the top of the mountain, we chose a tree that had a big, roomy crotch. "Now we will surprise the women," I laughed. "We will have the sho-kwin all made when they come back from gathering the rose fruits."

"You don't build the sho-kwin all at once!"

said Hutl-yah-mi-yuck. "You twist the willow branches into a flat circle for the base, and then you build up the sides just enough to hold one batch of acorns.

"Then some other time you build up the sides a little more to hold another batch, and then a little more. Why, we shall spend several days making this sho-kwin. When it is all done, we shall make a round top for it."

Again I was disappointed. It took so long to make Indian things! But all the rest of my life I should be thankful that I had learned the lesson of patience from the Indians. But how I hated patience now!

We twisted a large circle for the base of the sho-kwin and built a little fence around it. Then we raced off to gather acorns. After I had taken many trips for the acorns and dumped them into the sho-kwin, I began to see why the Indians didn't fill the basket right away. It was an endless job to fill it even to the rim of the little fence.

The crotch of the tree was low, so that we could pour the acorns into the sho-kwin without climbing into the tree.

I was so tired when night came that I crawled into my corner earlier than usual. But I couldn't go to sleep. I kept thinking about all the acorns I had gathered. Acorns and acorns and acorns!

## Hutl-yah-mi-yuck and I Weave a Basket

The fire was burning brightly in the middle of the hut. Op-a-chuck was sitting bolt upright on one side and Pi-on on the other.

"Tell me a story," I said to Pi-on. "Somehow I can't go to sleep."

Pi-on loved to tell stories. He remembered the stories that his father, the chief, had told him, and his father remembered the stories that his own father had told him before that.

"I will tell you the story of how the world began," he said, "and how the Indians got some sense."

## · 13 ·

# How the World Began

A LONG time ago two brothers lived away down in the earth. One brother had a badger with a pointed nose, and the other had a kit fox, a little animal with soft yellow hair that lives in the desert.

The older brother desired the animal with the soft yellow hair, but the younger brother would not give it to him.

So the older brother said to the younger brother, "Let us go to the top of the world to see what is there."

So the older brother closed his eyes and swam up through the water which covered the earth. When he reached the top he opened his eyes and looked about him. There was nothing but water.

Then the younger brother called up through the water and said, "How shall I come through the water?"

The older brother said: "Open your eyes and you can come through the water. But first let me hold your kit fox for you."

## How the World Began

So the younger brother opened his eyes and swam through the green water. He was blind when he reached the top.

Then the older brother handed the badger to him and said, "Here is your kit fox."

The younger brother felt of the fur and answered: "This is not my kit fox. This is your badger."

"No, it is not my badger. It is your kit fox."

"It is not my kit fox."

Then they quarreled, and the younger brother left the older brother and returned to his home under the sea. And whenever the earth shakes, it is because he is turning around in his sleep or moving his leg or waving his arm.

Now the older brother was all alone, sitting on the top of the water. He said to himself: "How can I dry up the ocean? I want some land around here."

He thought and he thought. Soon he had an idea. He called all the little red ants together. The little red ants brought up bundles of earth from below, piled up the land, and the water floated away.

Then he said to himself, "How am I going to make light?"

He thought and he thought. Then he made a moon out of silvery clay and threw the moon away up into the east, and it stuck there.

But the moon wasn't bright enough. So he made a cake of yellow clay and threw it into the east also. It was very bright. This was the sun.

Then he made some animals out of clay. He made soft, fluffy rabbits and bears and deer. But he wasn't pleased after he had made them.

"You animals don't work like people," he said to the animals, which were all sitting around in a ring. "I am going to make people that eat you."

And before the animals could say a word, he made a man out of mud and put breath in the man. He made a woman after that. Then he made lots of men and women. But he made only Indians.

Now the older brother became very sick one day and sent for a doctor.

The old medicine man walked over the mountain. His hair was long and white. He sucked the bad poison out of the older brother, and the poison turned into a pebble in his mouth.

Even then the sick man was not cured. He died within a few days. That is the reason why people die today. The Indians took him across the river and burned his body.

"Let us go home and think," said one of the people. "We can't stay like this always, never doing anything. We must have a feast when someone dies. We must build a large hut for all the people. We must have some kind of talk. We have no sense."

Then a wise man said: "There's a man down south called *Mi-hee-ah-wit-ah*,[1] which means: 'man who knows everything.' Who will go after him and bring him to us? One of you must go."

Then the bravest of the men spoke, "I will go if I must, but if I travel on the ground someone will eat me."

"Then change yourself into a willow seed that floats in the air like a feather," said the wise old man.

"Then I'll be seen," said the man.

"Then make yourself into a bubble and float down the river," said the other.

So he made himself into a shining bubble and floated down the river until he came to a *hum-il-kwah-taht* [2] sitting in the middle of the stream. He floated right into the mouth of the hum-il-kwah-taht, which is an animal that white people have never seen.

"Now I am in a fix," said the bubble. "How shall I get out? Must I stay here forever?"

But he found a little sharp stone in the hum-il-kwah-taht, and he cut a door in its body and sailed away.

[1] mī hē ah wĭt'ah.  [2] hŭm ĭl kwah taht'.

## Indians of the Oaks

After a peaceful journey on the water he reached the south. He floated to green land, turned himself into an Indian again, discovered the hut of Mi-hee-ah-wit-ah, and crawled through the roof, which was lightly thatched with brush.

"Who came?" asked a voice.

"Oh, I came," said the Indian.

"Well, what do you want?" asked the voice.

The Indian looked all around the hut, but he saw no one. Perhaps Mi-hee-ah-wit-ah had changed himself into a spider when he heard someone coming.

"What do you want?" repeated the voice.

"You know a lot of songs," said the Indian, feeling queer at talking aloud to someone he couldn't see. "We know nothing at all. We have no sense. We want you to teach us."

"All right," said Mi-hee-ah-wit-ah, "I will do that. Sorrowful is the man who has no sense. Tomorrow you will see me coming. You will see lots of dust. I have lots of feet. I will change myself into a shiny, hundred-legged centipede that will stretch from mountaintop to mountaintop. Build your hut big enough to hold me."

After he had listened to these words, the Indian changed himself into a bubble again and floated back to his home.

The next morning the Indians saw lots of dust.

## How the World Began

Mi-hee-ah-wit-ah stretched like a mighty snake from peak to peak. He left a track as he came along. That is why we see white patches on the rocks of these very mountains today.

Mi-hee-ah-wit-ah crawled through the thatched roof of the hut and coiled within the walls. No sooner had he done that than a mean Indian boy threw a lighted torch into the thatch, and the roof caught fire, and Mi-hee-ah-wit-ah was burned up!

And as he burned, chunks of his body flew in every direction, and the Indians swallowed the chunks! And after that they began to have some sense.

# 14

# The Tribe Gathers at Slanting Rock

"WE ARE going to the rocks today," said Op-a-chuck a few mornings later, as she put on her head a huge basket full of the dried acorn meats.

The rocks! the rocks! How often had I heard about the rocks! I could hardly wait to go.

All the women and children gathered together. Some of the women carried baskets on their heads, and some carried them in nets on their backs. All the baskets were full of acorn meats, ready to be ground in holes in the rocks. The children carried their acorn meats in little deerskin bags.

Hutl-yah-mi-yuck and I took only our bows and arrows, because we had to do all the hunting for the women that day, as the men had gone on a big deer hunt.

Op-a-chuck led us along a winding trail through the woods until we reached a sunny slope facing a deep green valley. The slope was called *Ah-wee-ah-pi-pah*,[1] which means "slanting rock."

All over Slanting Rock were deep holes which

[1] ah wē ah pī′ pah: *ah-wee*, rock; *ah-pi′pah*, slanting.

had been ground out by the great-great-grand-mothers of these very women.

"Hun! hun-nah! " cried the women, as they saw the rocks once more. "Hun! hun-nah!"

They separated and began running wildly around the foot of the rocks. Some of them pushed their arms into the hollows of trees, some of them poked into big cracks in the rocks with long sticks, and others began to dig in the soft matting of oak leaves which covered the ground.

"What are they doing?" I asked Hutl-yah-mi-yuck, as I looked at them with wonder in my eyes.

"Watch and you will see," answered Hutl-yah-mi-yuck, the wise one.

I watched them carefully, and soon I saw an old Indian woman pull out a long stone pestle from a hole in a tree. It was shaped like a thick club. All the other women began to find their pestles, too.

"They hide them every year," said Hutl-yah-mi-yuck. "They like to use only their own."

When the women had found their favorite pestles, they began to scramble up the sides of the rock and select their pet holes. Op-a-chuck picked out the deepest hole of all.

"She always grinds her acorns in that hole," said Hutl-yah-mi-yuck.

When all the women had taken their places, they poured some of the meats into their winnowing-

trays, rubbed the meats between the palms of their hands to loosen the skins, and winnowed the meats by shaking the basket up and down. The wind blew away the little red skins.

As soon as the acorn meats were clean, the women poured them into the holes and began to pound them with their pestles. *Chock, chock, chock!*

The squirrels peeked down from the branches and scolded loudly, so cross were they that their peaceful woods were disturbed. The blue jays flashed through the air overhead, calling "Hear! hear!" in their noisy language. All the birds fluttered near to see what could possibly have happened to their quiet woods.

## The Tribe Gathers at Slanting Rock

While the women were grinding the meal in the rocks, a little breeze crawled through the clearing and lifted some of the meal right out of the holes.

"*Mee-yip-ah!*" [1] (Listen to me!) called Op-a-chuck to Hutl-yah-mi-yuck and me. "The wind is stealing our meal. Build us some fences quickly!"

"Build fences!" Where? What could she mean? But I followed Hutl-yah-mi-yuck as if I knew what he was going to do.

Hutl-yah-mi-yuck ran down the slope until he came to some thick sage bushes. He ripped off many dry branches of these and rushed back to the rocks. I did the same.

He ran up the rocks and built little fences, or screens, around the holes to protect them from the wind. Then he set big stones on top of these thick fences to weigh them down.

"Now we can grind our meal without any trouble," said Op-a-chuck, as she started pounding again.

I hunted in the hollows of the oak trees until I found a stone pestle; then I chose a nice hole in Slanting Rock and sat down before it.

I winnowed my acorn meats as well as I could in Op-a-chuck's winnowing-tray; then I poured the meats into the hole and began to grind them. It seemed easy at first, but soon my back ached so

[1] mē yĭp′ah.

much that I thought it would break in two. But I noticed that the women were not resting or complaining, and I felt ashamed.

Then I discovered that they were sitting much straighter than I. They were bending from the waists only. After I learned to bend this way my back did not hurt so much.

Soon the Indians began to scoop out the meal with their hands and pour it into winnowing-trays. This time I asked no questions, but I watched Op-a-chuck very closely.

She shook the basket many times, until heavy lumps of meal rose to the top. These lumps had not been ground so fine as the rest. She scraped the lumps back into the grinding hole again, and ground them until the meal was as soft as the other. Then she added it to the first.

I tried to winnow my meal, too; but as I jerked the basket up and down, the meal fell all over my bare knees, and I lost every bit of it.

"H'm-m!" I said to myself, scrambling down the rock again. "This is woman's work, anyway. These women will have no supper if I do not kill some quail for them."

I started toward a little green valley with my bow and arrow. Hutl-yah-mi-yuck was kneeling at the edge of a pool, bathing his face. At his belt hung almost two dozen quail.

## The Tribe Gathers at Slanting Rock

"You are always doing what I am always saying," I said, sitting down on a rock and putting my head in my arms. I was getting discouraged in my hope of being as smart as an Indian.

Hutl-yah-mi-yuck turned his head slowly. I could feel his eyes upon me. Then he said: "Let the women grind their acorn meal. But it is well for you to try to do it once. I learned once, too. When my grandmother gets rheumatism, I grind the meal for her. But, k'yu! These quail won't be enough for everybody."

"You wait!" I said. "I will get as much game as you!"

But not until suppertime did I see the wood rats hanging on the other side of his belt. Hutl-yah-mi-yuck was still smarter than I!

# 15

# A Bitter Breakfast Mush

THE NEXT morning I crawled out of my little corner of our hut and tiptoed over to the basket of meal which Op-a-chuck had hung from the roof, out of the way of mice. I stepped up on a rock and pulled down the basket.

"Now I am going to have a feast," I said to myself. "It will take only a few minutes to cook this meal."

I put a little of it in a deerskin sack, hung up the basket again, and carried my sack outdoors. I poured the meal into a little olla, added water to it, and put the olla over a fire which I had made.

The meal began to cook. I could see it bubbling round the edge of the olla. I stirred it with the big oak spoon that Op-a-chuck always used. It grew thicker and thicker.

While I was watching my mush, Hutl-yah-mi-yuck walked along with his bow and arrow. A few quail hung from his belt. He stopped beside me and stared into the little cooking-olla.

"Are you going to eat that shah-wee?" he asked.

## A Bitter Breakfast Mush

"Of course I am going to eat it," I answered quickly. I thought that I had been very clever.

He said nothing, but walked along to his little brush hut, where his mother was already starting a fire.

When the mush was very thick, I dished it into a clay bowl, blew upon it to cool it, and dipped my first and second fingers into it because we had no spoons. At the very first taste of the mush I spit it out of my mouth. It was very bitter.

I was much disappointed, because I had heard the Indians talk so much about the shah-wee that I thought it was going to be very good food. I scraped the rest of the mush out of the olla and threw it away.

I heard a soft laugh behind me, and there stood Op-a-chuck, smiling at me.

"Not good?" she asked me.

"No!" I answered in her own language.

She laughed again. "K'yu!" she said. "I shall cook your breakfast."

I followed her into the hut. Fat quail were roasting in the ashes. Pi-on was poking them out with a stick.

"But I thought you were going to eat mush too," I cried.

"We will eat the mush when the mush is ready to eat," said Op-a-chuck. "Not before."

I did not know what she meant, but I asked no questions. I had learned to wait and see.

After breakfast Op-a-chuck called me into the sunshine under a tall oak tree.

"Get me some dry brush," she said.

I gathered a big pile of it.

"You have enough for the whole tribe," she said with a smile. "Take some of it to the mother of Hutl-yah-mi-yuck. She will need some, too." I started to carry some brush over there, when I saw Hutl-yah-mi-yuck carrying a bundle to his hut.

"He always does things before I can do them," I said to myself. So I carried the brush to an old woman who had no one to fetch and carry for her.

"Now make me a hawk's nest," said Op-a-chuck.

"A hawk's nest!" I cried. "But the hawk should have her nest in the top of a tree!"

"Not this hawk," said Op-a-chuck.

## A Bitter Breakfast Mush

So I made a hawk's nest on the ground. It was a big circle of brush.

"Now fetch me some water, my basket of meal, and my *n'yah-pun*," [1] said Op-a-chuck. The n'yah-pun is a basket so loosely woven that it has many tiny holes in it. It is a strainer.

Op-a-chuck put the n'yah-pun in the center of the hawk's nest, and then she mixed a little meal and water into a thick paste. She plastered the inside of the n'yah-pun with this paste until she had choked up all the holes.

[1] n'yah pūn'.

When it was nicely lined inside she filled it with meal and covered the meal with water, which she let fall, drop by drop, through her fingers. Then she sat straight up by the old tree trunk, rested her hands on her knees, and waited.

It took a long time for the water to run out of the basket. When it ran out it was red.

I was waiting, too. How peaceful it seemed in the forest! The golden leaves looked cheerful, and the earth was warm where the sun touched it. Blue smoke from campfires floated through the trees and trailed far away into the blue sky. Figures of Indian women knelt over their work. Children played quietly, gathering sticks for little playhouses. Hunters walked among the oaks, and a young woman followed the trail to the spring with a water olla on her head.

It seemed to me the happiest scene in the world. I wondered if it would always last, season after season.

"Hun!" said Op-a-chuck, suddenly. "*N'yah-mah!*[1] (Enough) Now it is ready to cook. Put your finger in it."

I poked my finger into the shah-wee and sucked my finger. "It is sweet!" I cried.

"Yes, it is sweet," said Op-a-chuck. "The bitterness ran away with the water."

[1] n'yah'mah.

## A Bitter Breakfast Mush

She picked up an acorn from the ground, shelled it, and then nibbled it. "Bitter!" she said, throwing it away. "The Indians learned years ago how to take the bitterness out of the acorns."

"And when shall we cook it?" I asked.

"Tonight," she said. "Tonight, when it is warm in the hut, and the fire is bright, and we are hungry and ready to eat. We shall have a feast tonight."

"May Hutl-yah-mi-yuck eat with us, too?" I asked.

"He may eat with us if he wants to eat with us," said Op-a-chuck. "Ask him."

So when night came Op-a-chuck and Pi-on and Hutl-yah-mi-yuck and I sat close to the fire, and I ate shah-wee for the first time. No, no! For the second time! And the second time I found it good!

And after we had eaten our supper of deer meat and shah-wee, Hutl-yah-mi-yuck and I curled up on the rabbitskin blanket, Op-a-chuck sat straight as always, and Pi-on told us several little Indian stories of the long ago.

# ‣ 16 ‣

## *The Good Green Ball That Grew from a Seed*

ONE COOL morning in autumn an old Indian woman walked along the bank of a creek. She was very, very old. Her hair was white and ragged. She had pulled some of it out because it blew in her eyes. These poor old eyes were so pale and dim that they looked as though they were under water. Her skin was wrinkled like an old squash skin.

But she had the nose of a coyote for sniffing things on the breeze, and her ears were as sharp as those of a wildcat. She carried an oak stick in her hand.

She had told the tribe that she was going to hunt for that strange thing she had smelled in the night. The wind had carried the sweet smell to her on its back.

She walked along the creek bank with her stick and feebly climbed over fallen boughs. She dodged the leaves of the poison oak and circled round the thorny bushes. After a while she saw a big green

ball on the sand, with vines running away from it.
The old woman stopped and looked at it silently.

"Aha!" she said to herself. "This is the strange
thing I smelled last night. It was this green ball!"

She threw down her stick and knelt on the sand.
She sniffed the ball and twisted it off its stem. It
was very shiny, as if it were wet. She carried it
back to the village.

All the Indians were sitting around in a circle.
They were playing a game with little painted sticks.
They threw down the sticks when she came near
them and looked at her with much surprise.

"What is it?" they cried, all pointing at the
green ball.

The old woman put the ball on top of a big rock.
All the Indians gathered round it. Never had
they seen anything like that.

Then the old woman spoke: "Last night the
wind brought me a strange smell on its back. I
had never smelled anything like it before — a cold,
sweet smell. It was this green ball.

"Not one of us has ever seen this ball before. It
may be good for us to eat. Or it may kill us all.
No one knows. If it is good we shall save the seeds
— if there are any seeds — and put them in the
ground. Then, perhaps, other balls will grow.

"I think that the white people have planted
seeds somewhere, and that some of the seeds

that they have planted have washed down the creek, and that this green ball has grown from a seed."

All the Indians looked at her in silence. They were scared. They were afraid that she would ask them to eat the new green ball. And they respected the wishes of old people.

## The Good Green Ball That Grew from a Seed

Then the old woman picked up a long stone pestle that lay at her feet. And she said: "I am a very old woman. I am the oldest woman in the tribe. If I die, it doesn't matter, because it will be time for me to die soon, anyway. I am going to break open the green ball and eat a piece of the inside."

So saying, she let the pestle fall with a *whack!* right on the ball, breaking it into many pieces. The pieces rolled all over the rock. The inside of the ball was soft and pink and juicy. The seeds looked like black beetles. The old woman put her fingers into the soft pink mush and licked them, and then quickly lay down on the earth because she thought she was going to die.

But she jumped up right away and cried: "It's sweet! It's sweet! It's good! Good! Hun! hun-nah!"

Then all the other Indians ran up to her and dipped their fingers into the soft pink mush, and sucked their fingers, and cried: "Hun! hun-nah!"

And that's the story of the first watermelon that the Indians ever tasted.

# ▸ 17 ◂

## *Mountaintop Stories*

---

THESE ARE the other stories that Pi-on told us in the warm little hut up on the mountaintop.

### THE OLD MAN WHO LIVED IN A SPRING

In the center of a green valley between high mountains there was a spring of hot water. Standing in the center of the spring, about waist-high, was an old, old Indian man with very long white hair hanging about his shoulders.

The Indians were afraid of this old man because he seized young Indian boys and girls who happened to wander near the spring and drew them down into the earth. But if the Indians did not call the old man by his name, he would not harm them. His name was *Hah-ro*,[1] which means "hot water."

One day an Indian mother was walking in the green valley with her little daughter. When she drew near the spring, she whispered to the little girl, "Now, my daughter, do not call the name of

[1] hah rō'.

the old man when you go by, for he will draw you down through the water into the earth."

So they walked along very softly; but just as they were passing the spring the young daughter called out, against her own wishes: "Hah-ro! Hah-ro!"

Instantly a great cyclone, or wind, came, and the girl caught hold of a manzanita[1] bush, and the cyclone ripped up the manzanita bush and carried the bush and the young daughter high into the air.

[1] mahn sa nē'ta.

Then it swept them down toward the spring, and a quick-rising mist hid them from sight.

When the mist cleared, the mother looked all around her, and she saw only the mountains far off and the green valley and the bubbles of the spring.

Even the old man was gone.

He had sucked the manzanita bush and the young daughter into the earth.

## HOW THE SNAKES LOST THEIR TEETH

Once upon a time all the snakes had teeth. They all could bite.

One day an inchworm, a curious little worm that humps himself up as he walks, crawled across the trail down which the snakes were wriggling. The snakes stared at the inchworm, a creature which they had never seen before, and he seemed so funny to them that some of them began to laugh.

They laughed and they laughed. And while their mouths were wide open their teeth dropped out. But the ones that didn't laugh kept their teeth. And these are the rattlesnakes with the bad bite.

## WHY THE WHITE MAN LOOKS COLD

There is one kind of bee that lives in the earth in the desert. It is called the "desert queen bee."

The north queen bee is white, the east queen

bee is red, the south queen bee is yellow, and the west queen bee is black.

And so the Indians always say that the color of the cold north is white, that the color of the sunrise in the east is red, that the color of the warm south is yellow, and that the color of the rain in the west is black.

And if you ask an Indian how he likes the white skin of a white man, he will say, "Cold! cold!"

# The White Arrowhead

WHEN MORNING came the sky grew cloudy, and Pi-on said to the tribe: "It is going to snow. We must hurry back to our village."

Somehow I didn't want to go. I wanted to stay! Stay! I wanted once more to grind the acorns at Slanting Rock. I wanted once more to run down to the willows where Hutl-yah-mi-yuck and I had cut branches for the sho-kwin.

I looked all around me. I saw the women putting on their basket caps and heavy nets. I saw the men gathering up their bows and arrows, which they had stacked against the oaks. I saw the children climbing the branches for the last time and hiding among the leaves.

One old woman under an old oak tree was cracking her last nuts in a stone bowl, or mortar, which she kept on the mountaintop. She was using a thick pestle. She didn't like to work at the rock holes with all the other women. She liked to work alone.

"Now, now, while they are all getting ready to

leave," I thought, "I can run over to Slanting Rock for one last look. Once again I want to feel the old stone pestle in my hand. Once again I want to smell the willows."

I crawled into our little shelter, picked up a deerskin sack of acorns which I had gathered and cracked and dried, and dashed around the edge of the oak grove. Then, when I was beyond the spreading trees and the vine tangles underfoot, I ran like a deer to Slanting Rock.

How quiet it was there! The rocks shone gray under the gray sky, and the leaves were dark gold above them. I hunted for Op-a-chuck's big pestle. She had hidden it in a deep crack in a rock. "*How-ka!*" [1] I said softly to the pestle, for it seemed like an old friend. *How-ka* means "hello." It is the greeting word of the Indians.

"How-ka! how-ka!" I lifted the pestle. How heavy it was! How strong Op-a-chuck was to handle this thick stone!

Hugging it closely, so that it would not drop on my bare toes, I carried it to her favorite hole. I put it down, poured a few of my acorn meats into the hole, and began to pound softly.

I had not been pounding long when a strange feeling came over me. "This is the last time you will do this," something seemed to say. I pounded

[1] how'ka.

only once or twice after that, and then I took the pestle back to the rock and hid it exactly where it had lain before.

"Now I will take a last look at the patch of willows," I said to myself. I ran lightly down the slope, and the cool smell of moist willows reached me. "Ah!" I thought. "Soon these willow branches will be covered with snow. I will take one now, before it is white."

I broke off a little branch and stuck it into my braided belt. It poked into my skin a little, but I didn't mind. My skin was growing tough.

Then I stood still and thought — what, what is the last and best thing that I want to do on the mountaintop? It was a funny answer that came to me. The last and best thing that I wanted to do was to lie down on the sweet earth with my cheek against the fallen leaves. I lay there a long time.

And then I heard a voice. It seemed away off. Kwee-tahk! Kwee-tahk! It was a low, deep voice, like night wind in the woods. I lifted my head and tossed my hair away from my ears.

It was the voice of Op-a-chuck.

"Kwee-tahk! Kwee-tahk! K'yu! k'yu! k'yu!" she called.

I hopped to my feet, scrambled up the slope, dashed by Slanting Rock, and soon I stood by her side.

## The White Arrowhead

"Where were you?" she asked. And then she saw the willow branch in my belt, and she nodded her head. Then she saw the deerskin sack of acorn meats, and she nodded her head again. And then she saw the earth on my cheek and the twigs in my hair, and she nodded again. She smiled a slow smile this time. She understood why I loved the earth mother.

The tribe was ready to go. The men were already starting single file down the mountain, their bows and arrows in their hands or sticking from quivers on their backs. The quivers were new ones of wildcat, coyote, or badger skins.

"Where is Pi-on?" I asked Op-a-chuck, as she hung a heavy net between her shoulder blades.

"Look about you," said she. "If you were lost in the desert, would you say to the rocks 'Where is Pi-on?'" But she smiled when she said it.

I looked about me. I saw Pi-on bending over our campfire. He was covering it with earth. Over the ashes he threw twigs and leaves and pieces of pine bark. Never did Pi-on like to leave a trace of where he had been.

While I was watching Pi-on, Hutl-yah-mi-yuck walked silently by me.

"Do you want this?" he asked, stretching out his hand.

I looked into his brown palm. In its hollow

shone something white. It was a perfect little arrowhead of shining white stone. It was chipped finely along the edges.

"I found it at Slanting Rock," he said, "the day you were grinding acorns with the women. I wanted to keep it then, but now I will give it to you."

"Why do you want to give it to me now?" I asked in a wondering voice.

"Because you have not found one yourself," he answered simply.

## The White Arrowhead

How did he know that I hadn't found one myself? These Indians seemed to guess everything.

I took the arrowhead from his hand and put it
carefully into my deerskin bag. I didn't say "Thank
you," because the Indians never said it. They
have no words for "Thank you." I knew that I
should keep the arrowhead forever.

Hutl-yah-mi-yuck then left me and joined the
men. He carried his bow and arrows in his hand
and watched every flutter in the bushes.

Pi-on walked up to Op-a-chuck and me and said
something to Op-a-chuck which I couldn't hear.
She lifted the heavy net from her shoulders, and he
hung it over his. Then she set on her back a lighter
net of her camping things. They fell into line.

"My own Indians are the best," I thought.
"They are the kindest toward one another. One
thinks of the other, and the other thinks of the
one." They turned to see if I were following, and
they both smiled at me. I smiled back.

When we reached the spring beside the trail we
all stopped to take a drink of the cool fresh water.
I waited a little while behind the others because I
saw a strange red flower that I wished to pick.
The flower grew in a crack of a rock near the trail.

As I leaned over the flower I felt someone seize
me, and before I could cry out to Pi-on a hand
was clapped over my mouth and I was carried to

a mountain road not far away. I looked up into the face above me. It was the face of the bad rancher from whom I had run away.

The rancher drove me to a railway station and sent me on a train to another state — almost another land, it seemed to me. It was his brother's home to which he sent me. But his brother was kind and good, and I lived with him as his son for many years.

Pi-on! Op-a-chuck! This is the way I was taken from you. Is this the reason you felt you would be unhappy in your new home, Op-a-chuck? Did you know I wouldn't be there to sleep in my dark little corner?

How often I think of that morning when the old woman dragged me into the sunlight, and the strange tribe of Indians stood around me. How clearly come the words of my father again and again, "Experience is good, my son, whether it is pleasant or unpleasant."

My experience with the Indians of the Oaks was pleasant. It was almost a dream. Only the white arrowhead of Hutl-yah-mi-yuck tells me that it was true.

▶▶▶  ◀◀◀

# Secrets

# of the

# Trail

# ▸ 1 ◂

# *The Herbwoman and Her Baby*

---

IT HAPPENED so long ago that she couldn't remember anything about it. She had been such a tiny baby then. How could she remember that she had been fastened to a cradle?

But the old owl in the deep hole in the tree remembered. He had seen her go by many times, many times. She rode on the back of the herbwoman. She was wrapped in an Indian cradle, and a shade of woven bark protected her eyes from the bright sunlight.

If the herbwoman was looking at the mountains, the brown eyes of the baby were looking at the green valley. If the herbwoman was looking at the valley, the brown eyes of the baby were looking at the mountains.

The baby never looked the way the mother looked. How could it, when it was strapped to a cradle that hung on its mother's back?

Every morning the herbwoman walked up the mountain trail. She was always searching for medicines and medicines and medicines.

She was always looking for seeds and roots and leaves that make the eyes shine as clearly as pebbles under water. She was always looking for plants that make the lips glow like wild cherries.

She was the giver of health and the keeper of health. All the Indians listened to her words She was the herbwoman.

One morning the herbwoman started up the trail in the early sunlight. Her baby lay in the cradle as usual, its eyes looking toward the valley below. From the floor of the valley rose many thatched huts. The smoke from fires sifted through the thatch. Indians walked busily to and fro.

## The Herbwoman and Her Baby

Up and up climbed the herbwoman. She wore
a little skirt of willow-bark strips. Her long black
hair fell almost to her knees. A red circle was
painted on each cheek. In the circle was a white
dot. On her head she carried a large seed basket.
The bottom of the basket rested on a ring of bark.
She walked as easily as if she carried no basket on
her head.

She stopped at a little clearing by the trail. The
clearing was a rock ledge, but the rock only showed
in places. It was mostly covered by a thin layer
of moss and grasses. Above and below the ledge
many plants were growing.

The herbwoman took off her basket and let the
ring slip down her hair. She lifted the cradle from
her back and hung it on the bough of a sweet-
smelling sumac bush.

Little insects flew about the baby's cheeks, and
it began to cry. So the herbwoman blew them all
away and threw a little net of fiber thread over the
shade of the cradle. She had woven the net for
just this purpose. The baby wasn't bothered now,
so it fell asleep.

As soon as the herbwoman had settled her baby
nicely, she began the tasks of the morning. She
had many things to do.

The old medicine man, her father, had asked her
to dig him some roots. He wanted to save the

roots for some desert Indians who were coming all the way from the desert to fetch them. And he wanted some for himself.

And she wanted to gather some blossoms for her old, old grandmother, who was so old that she looked like a furry owl. And the three old sisters in the hut in the wild-rose patch were crying for fresh and nice things to nibble. They had eaten all the sweet rose fruit in the wild-rose patch.

The herbwoman untied a long digging stick from her belt. She never went anywhere without this

## The Herbwoman and Her Baby

stick, for she never knew where she might find some herb. It was quite worn at the end, but she sharpened it often.

She scrambled off the rock ledge and knelt down by some wild-peony plants. The red flowers were just coming into bud. She pushed her digging stick away down under one plant. The stick slid nicely into the soft dark earth. She poked up the plant gently; then another and another plant. She broke off the stems and saved only the roots.

She wrapped the roots in the fringed peony

leaves, so that they would not dry, and carefully tucked them into a corner of her basket. Then she gathered many more of the same roots.

"These roots are good when one has a sharp pain inside," she said to herself. "No matter how great the pain, the roots will stop it. I think the pain comes from eating the wrong things. My father, the medicine man, can stew some of these roots for himself and save the rest for the desert people."

Then the herbwoman looked about for something to ease the rheumatism of her old, old grandmother.

"H'm-m!" she said to herself. "If she hadn't stood in the wet marshes all day, picking the basket grass, she wouldn't have rheumatism. And if she hadn't gone up the mountain in the storm and lain in the cold cave all night, she wouldn't have rheumatism. H'm-m! It is better to think once first than twice last. But how can I keep her at home?"

As she was wondering what she should gather, a little vine tickled her neck. Looking around her, she found the snowy flowers of clematis, or old-man's-beard.

"Here you are!" she said. "I didn't expect to find you away up here. Some little animal has carried your seed in his coat and shaken it off in this soft earth." So saying, she gathered great bunches of the white flowers and tucked these into her basket, too.

## The Herbwoman and Her Baby

"And what will my old, old grandmother do when I give her these blossoms?" she asked herself. (Herbwomen often talk to themselves.) "And what will she do? She will stew the blossoms in the big olla with the wide mouth, and then she will stick her feet in the olla and put them to soak.

"And I must tell her again, because she always forgets. She never used to forget, and she was the very one who taught me the secret, but now she always forgets. I must tell her to soak her legs once and then wait for three days. Then soak her legs again and wait for three days. Then soak her legs again and wait for three days. If she doesn't do exactly that, she won't get well."

Then the herbwoman said many words to herself that even the listening birds couldn't hear. She was thinking out loud about all the things she told sick Indians to do. She was thinking how sometimes they forgot one little thing which kept them from getting well. "All things or none," she said.

It was easy to gather fresh bits for the three old sisters to nibble. Fresh leaves were growing on every plant. But not all fresh leaves were good to eat. She chose the leaves with care. She nipped off with her fingernails the tender young ends of the white sage, the most useful plant of the Indians.

She loved the white sage better than all the other

plants. It was such a friendly plant. It gave so many gifts. It gave tender young leaves to nibble. It gave tiny, tiny seeds to roast for breakfast mush. It gave soft leaves that smelled sweet when they were burning. In the steam of these leaves all pain and sorrow melted away.

She looked about for other fresh greens. She nipped off the pointed, juicy leaves of the stone-crop. This little plant grew in the crack of a rock. Its stems looked like babies' fingers. The fingers were rosy at the ends.

She knelt down in a marshy spot by a hidden spring and plucked many leaves of miner's lettuce. This gay little plant pokes its brave stem right through the leaf, so that the stem, with the leaf on top, looks like a parasol.

The herbwoman nibbled one of the leaves herself. "It is bitter and cool," said she. "The three old sisters will like these leaves."

She did not toss the herbs into her basket in any way. She tied each kind of herb into a neat bundle. She tied it with cattail string that was growing in the marshy spot. She made the string by splitting a cattail leaf with her fingernails and making it soft with her wet fingers.

She was like a real doctor, and she couldn't keep her things in a mess. She kept them all separate. She didn't have to label them, because she knew what they all were. Everybody else knew what they were, too, but everybody else didn't know how to use them. She wouldn't know how to label them either, even if she had wished to. She couldn't write and she couldn't draw.

"I have gathered enough for this morning," she said at last. "I will hand them out while they are still fresh."

She covered the herbs in her basket with large cool leaves. She gently lifted the cradle from the bough and swung the cord over her forehead.

She was not wearing a basket cap, which would keep the cord of the cradle from cutting into her forehead, because she was carrying a seed basket on her head. So she wadded her hair under the cord to keep it from cutting. With the ring on top of her head and the basket on top of that, she looked across the valley.

She stood on one mountain and she looked across at another mountain. On the other side of the mountain opposite snuggled another Indian village. She could not see it, but she knew it was there. She knew she should pass near it when she traveled to the piñon[1] country in the early fall.

"I wish it were fall now," she said to herself, smacking her lips.

She started down the trail. She lifted her chest

[1] pē nyōn'.

so that she could stand perfectly straight. If she didn't stand straight she couldn't carry the basket on her head. If she couldn't carry the basket, she couldn't carry the herbs home without a lot of fuss.

She walked down the trail. She did not have far to go because she had not gone far in the beginning.

"It does not matter how far one goes, but what one does on the way," she said to herself.

As she looked down the trail the brown eyes of the baby were looking up the trail. The mother eyes and the baby eyes never looked the same way at the same time.

# ⟩ 2 ⟨

## *In the Meadow Marshes*

SOMETIMES THE herbwoman wandered in the meadow marshes early in the morning. The marshes followed along the creek waters, lapping up the ripples that flowed over.

Summertime found many plants in flower. Spring rains and warm sunshine opened their petals. Springtime in the land of the *Kum-mee-is*[1] is the time of rain, whether it rains in November or December or later.

When the rain comes the spring comes. And the brown thrasher, — the bird with the long, curved bill that sings like a mockingbird, — the brown thrasher always tells the Indians when rain is coming.

One summer morning the herbwoman put on her basket cap and carrying-net, the cords of which crossed over the cap. Then she tucked the cradle and baby under her arm and marched off toward the lizardtail patches.

Now these lizardtails are not real lizard tails.

[1] kŭm mē īs'.

[ 129 ]

They are plants with thick, stubby flowers that look like lizard tails.

The ground was so damp that the herbwoman hung her baby on the bough of a buttonball, or sycamore, tree. The sun shone in the baby's eyes. So the mother plucked a large sycamore leaf and fastened it with a little stick to the shade of the cradle. The woven shade of the cradle was too narrow to hide all the sun.

"When I make another cradle, I will make a broader shade," said the herbwoman.

She dug the roots of the lizardtails with her digging stick and lined her net with sycamore leaves. Then she filled her net with roots. She had not brought her seed basket this morning.

As she bent over the net, filling it with the roots, a beautiful little water snake slipped over her bare feet. She did not move. She was not afraid of any snake except the rattlesnake. She even hunted for rattlesnakes, because the oil was good for rheumatism. She always kept an earthen jar of rattlesnake oil for old people.

Rattlesnakes were good to eat, too. They were sweet and tender. They were very nice when boiled, but they did not smell nice while they were cooking.

While the herbwoman was thinking about good things to eat she began to hear a steady humming

over her head. She looked up into the branches of
the tree and saw one little golden-brown bee. The
bags on its legs were stuffed with blue pollen from
flowers. The little bee flew straight into a crack
in the tree trunk. Another bee flew in, too; then
another; then another.

The baby cradle was hanging very near the bee
hole. For a moment the herbwoman thought she
would take it away. Then she thought, "The bees
are too busy to disturb my baby, and my baby is
too quiet to disturb them." So she left the baby
hanging there.

She knew everything about wild bees. She was
not afraid to gather a whole colony in her lined net
when it swarmed. She wondered why there were
more bees than there used to be. She did not know
that the white people had brought bees to the land
of the Kum-mee-is. Many of these bees had flown
away to the wild forest.

In the marshes grew a tall clover. The herbwoman gathered many sprays of this clover. It
filled her net to overflowing. "Every Indian man
and woman and child should eat this clover often,"
said she. "I will gather it for the whole tribe."
She decided to cook some of it right then.

"My Yuma[1] cousin has been eating too much
acorn mush," she said. The Yuma cousin had

[1] yōō′ma.

never tasted acorn mush before, and she liked it so well that she didn't know when to stop eating.

"She needs a meal of this clover. I will cook some for her. If everybody knew all the secrets of the woods, I should not have to do all these things."

But she smiled to herself. She was glad that everybody didn't know the secrets. She liked to be a doctor.

She walked into the wettest part of the marshes until she found a patch of tall reeds. They were not the reeds that the Indians used for weaving their seed baskets. They were very thin, soft reeds with brown seedcases.

They were used in making the Indian's basket-strainer. Except the basket cap, that is the only basket for which they could be used. The herb-woman needed a basket-strainer to cook her clover.

She did not split the reeds. She did not soak them. She sat right down on a little dry hill and twisted them very loosely into a basket just as they were. She couldn't have done a thing with them if they had not been fresh.

"I guess I will stay here all day," she said to herself. "I like it here."

It took her the rest of the morning to make her basket. It took many days to make a seed basket.

"It has taken most of my day," she said; "but

it will last me for many moons, if I don't have to give it away." She smiled.

Many of the women couldn't make nice basket-strainers. Some of them made beautiful ollas, some of them made beautiful winnowing-trays for winnowing acorn meal, and some of them made beautiful willow-bark skirts. But very few of them made everything well.

The herbwoman couldn't make a very nice olla herself. She really didn't have time to practice because she was gathering herbs all day long. She made a beautiful job of that.

Now she kindled a fire from a smoking piece of oak punk that she carried in a little olla. She didn't want to bother to use her two sticks, with which she could make fire, all the time. It took lots of strength to use these sticks. It was really a man's job, but she had no man in her family. Her husband had been killed in a war with the enemies of her tribe.

She coiled the clover into a cooking-olla which she had left upside down among the roots of a sycamore tree. She often made a campfire on this little dry hill, so she kept her olla handy. She filled the olla almost to the brim with fresh water from the creek. She put it on three stones which she had placed round the fire.

In a short while the water began to bubble.

## Secrets of the Trail

The greens were cooking! Soon she had an olla full of stewed greens. She didn't cook them too long. She cooked them just enough.

But there is always too much water left in stewed greens. So she lifted the greens out of the water with a willow stick. She dropped them into her new basket, which she had placed on a nest of leaves. Then she pressed out the water with her stick. The water ran through the holes. "My basket-strainer works very nicely," she said.

When the greens were dry enough and yet not too dry, she stored them in her net. She said to herself that a big bowl of greens was the best thing that anybody could eat. It was good food and good medicine too.

She looked about her for a few more things to take home. She still had some of the day left for hunting. She covered the fire with ashes and silently tiptoed over to her baby. The baby was just waking from a long, long nap.

The herbwoman lifted the cradle off the branch — very carefully, because the bees were thicker than ever — and sat down on a fallen bough with the baby on her lap. She unfastened it from the cradleboard and let it kick its feet and wave its arms. Then she fed it and hung the cradle on another branch.

The herbwoman hunted through the marshes until she had collected enough things to satisfy her. She found some barred feathers of a hawk that had been caught by a wildcat. She picked them up carefully and smoothed them out. "I will give these to the boys in the village for their arrows," she said.

Then she found a piece of red stone called jasper. The stone looked as if an Indian had started to make an arrow point of it and never finished his task. "Perhaps he had to go away to war," thought the herbwoman. "It might have been the same war in which my husband was killed.

"I will give this stone to the medicine man, and maybe he will finish making it into an arrow point. But maybe he won't. Perhaps it will make him sad to touch something that some unhappy Indian could not finish."

So saying, she put the stone back on the ground and felt sorry that she had touched it herself.

She began to think so much about this unhappy Indian that she started the fire again. She threw some white-sage branches into it and stood in the sweet-smelling steam. As the steam flowed over her body and drifted into her nose all sad thoughts floated away. She felt as happy as she had felt early in the morning.

She thought that she had better go home while she was feeling happy. So she put out the fire, gathered up the ends of her net, unhooked the baby cradle from the bough, and started home.

She tucked the cradle under her arm again.

## In the Meadow Marshes

Sometimes she carried her baby and its cradle on her head too. It all depended on what other things she carried on her back or what she carried on her head or in her hands. But whichever way she carried the baby, the baby liked it. Ever since it was born it had ridden with its mother up the trail and down the meadow.

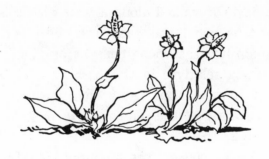

# ▸ 3 ◂

## *The Yuma Cousin and the Cactus*

IN THE late summer the herbwoman hunted for fruits of the cactus. This was the tuna[1] cactus. The fruit is called cactus pear. She took a companion with her when she gathered the cactus fruit. She always needed help then.

One day she walked along a trail with this companion. As usual the baby was with her. The companion was the young cousin from Yuma. She was visiting relatives in the herbwoman's village. She had more cousins there than just the herbwoman. Many of the Yumas were related to the Kum-mee-is.

The Yuma cousin was unhappy in the herbwoman's village because there was no river in which she could swim. She had strong shoulders for swimming and no place to swim. She had always lived on the Colorado River.

She thought the creeks and pools in the herbwoman's village were not wet enough. They were very dry in spots. But the herbwoman, who had

---

[1] tū'na.

### The Yuma Cousin and the Cactus

known nothing else, thought them very wet and flowing with sweet water. Besides, the herbwoman didn't know how to swim. She had never had a chance to learn.

Now the herbwoman and the Yuma cousin walked down the trail to a green meadow. Along the trail grew a stiff little plant called tarweed. It bore tiny yellow flowers. The herbwoman gathered a handful of stalks. The bunch of stalks looked just like a whisk broom.

She stored this whisk broom in her net, for she wore a basket cap and net that day. She carried her sleeping baby and its cradle on her arm.

The herbwoman and the Yuma cousin chatted happily as they walked along. The baby didn't know whether it liked all this chatting or not. It was used to riding with its mother only. Sometimes its mother talked softly to herself, but this *kwur-kwur*[1] was different.

Soon they came to a huge cactus. The flat, round lobes, which look like leaves, and the sharp white thorns were very ugly. The Yuma cousin cried "Ugh!" She was afraid to go too near. She wasn't used to cactus exactly like this.

But the herbwoman was not afraid. She had gathered cactus pears since she was a little girl. She circled round the green lobes until she found a small open space between the branches. She stepped closer. She brushed the pears with her whisk broom. This brushing loosened the spines. She turned her face away because if only one spine blew into her eye, it would blind it, she thought.

Then she asked the Yuma cousin to take the cactus bag out of the net.

The Yuma cousin reached down into the herb-

[1] kwur kwur': talk-talk.

## The Yuma Cousin and the Cactus

woman's net and pulled out a bag about a foot long. The bag looked like a little hammock with holes in it, except that it was all in one piece. It did not open flat like a hammock. It had a round hole at each end with drawstrings to close it.

The herbwoman broke off a twig from a sumac bush and bent it into a curve. Then she opened the two ends of the twig, as if they were scissors, and nipped the lower end of the pear between them. She pulled off the pear and dropped it into the bag which the Yuma cousin was holding. She gathered many of the fruits in this way.

"Now what shall I do?" asked the Yuma cousin, still holding the bag. She was not used to this sort of thing. She could do many things. She could make beautiful bead necklaces out of the beads that the white people gave her, but she didn't know a thing about the cactus pears in the land of the Kum-mee-is, although she knew about many other kinds of cactus fruits.

"Shake the bag from side to side," said the herbwoman. "Only then will all the little hairs drop off."

The Yuma cousin gently shook the bag from side to side.

"You do not do it quickly enough," said the herbwoman. "Here, take the baby."

She handed the cradle to the Yuma cousin, who took it gently, laughing all the time at the way she had handled the cactus bag. Her laughter was as low and sweet as the voice of a river. Perhaps the river had taught her how to laugh.

She was taller than the herbwoman, her shoulders were broader, and her hair was longer. She looked like a river woman; like a fine swimmer.

The herbwoman took the bag in both hands and quickly shook it sidewise until the cactus pears were free from spines.

"Now they are good to eat," she said. "We will eat them on the trail."

## The Yuma Cousin and the Cactus

The herbwoman took her baby again, and led the Yuma cousin down a little path to a place called *N'mee n'wah*,[1] "Home of the Wildcats." The Indians had seen many wildcats here.

Some other animal prints showed in the trail today. Little fresh fawn tracks showed clearly. It looked as if a fawn had just jumped away. The tracks were sliding.

"I think there is water near here," said the Yuma cousin, looking at the tracks. She was always sniffing for water.

"There is water near," said the herbwoman; "but I suppose *you* wouldn't call it water."

They came to a smooth ledge of rock. Branches of oak trees sheltered three sides of it. At its base shone a little pool. Weaving in and out of the pool were strips of sand. In the sand were the neat prints of a raccoon, a wildcat, and a skunk.

"The animals are out walking this morning," said the herbwoman.

The Yuma cousin looked right over the pool. Her eyes were hunting for greater things — the wide river of the Colorado and the farthest banks. She longed for a cooling swim.

The herbwoman guessed her thoughts. Indians do not have to speak every word to each other. Half of the words are in the air.

[1] n'mē' n'wah'.

[ 143 ]

"We will take a bath here," said she.

She hunted around for a safe place to put her baby. She was afraid to lay it down on the glassy rock for fear it would slide off. She was afraid to tuck it in a little cave close by, because a wildcat might be living there.

So she hung it up on a strong bough under a patch of oak leaves. They were the leaves of the scrub oak, a small kind of oak tree. She noticed tiny acorns upon the boughs.

"The acorns are still green," said she. "They will not be brown until two more moons. If there are no acorns on the black oak trees in the mountains, and if there are no acorns on the live oaks, we will use the little acorns of the scrub oaks. But most of the Indians have acorns left over from last year."

"I do not feel sorry for you," said the Yuma cousin. "You always have many things to eat. You have the piñon nuts, which are sweet and good, too, from the little pine trees in the forest. The Yumas live a harder life. The mesquite beans are almost all that we have — except little odds and ends."

"How do you prepare them?" asked the herb-woman, who had never been to Yuma.

"We pick them off the mesquite tree," said the Yuma cousin. "Then we grind them in wooden mortars with long stone pestles. Usually a man grinds them because the pestle is so long and heavy. He stands up instead of sitting down."

The herbwoman laughed. "All that seems so funny to me," she said. "A wooden mortar! Why don't you use stone?"

"Because we haven't so many rocks in the desert as you," said the Yuma cousin.

"And a man grinding up the beans! Why! that is woman's work!" said the herbwoman.

"It is too hard work for a woman," said the Yuma cousin. "But sometimes, when there is no man in the family, the woman uses a little mortar and a short pestle, and then she sits on the ground and grinds the beans."

"Ho! that sounds more like it," said the other. "And after the beans are ground, what then?"

"After the beans are ground we winnow them and dig a round pit in the earth and pour the meal into the pit. The meal stiffens into a cake. We break the cake into pieces and eat the pieces, or else we mix the pieces with water and drink them."

"H'm-m!" said the herbwoman. "I never heard of such a funny way of preparing a meal."

"Your way of cooking mush seems funnier to me," replied the Yuma cousin.

As they walked down the slope to the pool below

they both thought about all the queer ways and peoples in a queer world. They reached the edge of the pool. It seemed as if it were made just for the two of them. It was just deep enough and just wide enough for a great big bathtub.

But the Yuma cousin pouted her lips. "This is a funny swimming pool!" she said. "How can I move my legs or arms?"

"It is not a swimming pool," said the herb-woman a little crossly. "It is a bathing pool. And you are lucky to get even this on a hot day." She was out of patience with the fine ways of her Yuma cousin.

She slipped off her little willow-bark skirt and stepped into the pool. The Yuma cousin did the same.

The water was cool and fresh. The two women bathed their hot faces. They tossed the ripples at each other with their toes. They laid back their heads and let their hair float like seaweed. The water felt soft and delicious.

When they had cooled off enough, they sat on a rock ledge to get dry. They put on their little willow skirts again. The rock was covered with oak leaves that pricked into their skin. But they did not mind that. Many things pricked into their skin, because they never wore anything but their little skirts.

## The Yuma Cousin and the Cactus

While they were sitting on the rock they let the oak leaves fall through their fingers. Suddenly the Yuma cousin called out, "See what I have found!" She had uncovered a deep grinding-hole in the rock. "This is a hole for grinding acorns, isn't it?" she asked.

"Why, yes, it is!" cried the herbwoman. "And here is another, and another!"

"I guess some Indians lived here once," said the Yuma cousin. "There must be other things about here, too."

"I am certain of it," said the herbwoman, jumping from the rock. "Let us look for more things." She seized a stick and began poking about in the soft matting of oak leaves that covered the ground.

She found a broken clay pipe and a perfect little arrow point. She let them stay just where they were lying. She didn't touch them.

"Have you ever heard about this village?" asked the Yuma cousin.

"I heard once, but I had forgotten," she said. "Now I remember clearly. It was called *Wah ko-pi*,[1] 'House of the Poison Oak.' The Indians moved away because there was so much poison oak it bothered them. But if there were no poison oak, it would be just the right place for a village.

[1] wah kō pī'.

[ 147 ]

"It is sheltered from the wind. It has a high mountain at the north with many caves for hiding acorns. It has oak trees, basket grass, house thatch, and all good things. I should like to live here myself."

"But what should you do about the poison oak?" asked the Yuma cousin.

"I should burn it off."

"Maybe those other Indians tried that, too."

"Maybe."

They stood silently in the old-time village. Then the herbwoman said: "It is time to feed my baby. Let's go back to the ledge."

She walked up the rock and then over to the scrub-oak tree. The Yuma cousin followed. As the herbwoman slipped the cord of the cradle off the bough she felt something soft touching her hand. It was a hummingbird's nest of sycamore down. It looked as if one little bite had been taken out of the nest.

"A blue jay nipped this nest," said the herb-woman, who knew everything about birds. "He was after the eggs."

She fed her baby in the shelter of the tree.

"Have you any cactus pears left?" she asked her Yuma cousin. They had been nibbling them now and then.

"I have one," said the cousin.

## The Yuma Cousin and the Cactus

"And I have two," said the herbwoman. "We will give them to the three old sisters who live in the wild-rose patch. It is a little too far for them to walk here and gather them."

They followed the trail toward home, the herbwoman looking toward her village of thatched huts, and her baby looking back upon the trail over which they had passed.

# Wahss Surprises Her Mother

FOUR SUMMERS had come and gone, and the baby with the big brown eyes still had no name.

"How can I name her when the name hasn't come just right?" the herbwoman asked herself.

Very early one morning the baby toddled to the little arched doorway of the hut. A light mist floated over the valley. The tops of the Indian huts rose out of the mist like sawed-off tops of haystacks. The whole village looked as if it were sunk in a bowl of violet jelly.

The baby stopped in the doorway, looked about with wondering eyes, and then said one little word, "*Wahss!*" "Wahss" is the Indian name for "mist."

The herbwoman, who was tying some herbs into bundles, heard her baby say this little word. "Now the time has come," she said. "The name has found itself. I will call her Wahss." And so Wahss became her name.

Wahss always wanted to do exactly what her mother did. If her mother spread leaves in the sunshine, Wahss wanted to spread leaves, too. If her mother winnowed seeds in a basket, Wahss wanted to winnow seeds, too.

If her mother ground up acorn meats, . . . but Wahss couldn't do that, no matter how much she wished she could. The pestle was too heavy for her to hold. The old medicine man, her grandfather, promised to make a tiny bowl and pestle for her very own.

One day the herbwoman told Wahss that she was going up on the oak hill where the basket grass grew. Now there were two kinds of basket material that the Indians used for the outside of their baskets.

One kind of material was a reed that grew in the creek. The other was the twig of a bush that grew among young oaks. Of course there was the reed for the basket-strainer too, but that doesn't count. Sometimes the reed for the strainer was used for making basket caps.

It was the twig of a certain bush that the mother wished to get — the twig of the redberry, or squaw-bush. It made a stronger basket than the reed.

The herbwoman started walking across the meadow. She took no knife except her sharp fingernails, which were always with her.

Little Wahss toddled after her mother. Wahss had hair that grew low on her forehead and fell over her eyes. Her chubby brown body was as strong as that of a baby coyote.[1]

They crossed a little creek running happily through the meadow. A tiny strip of sand rose in the middle of it. On this sand lay a dead little hermit thrush. Its back was red-brown, and its breast was splashed with dots.

Baby Wahss ran over to the little bird and knelt down beside it. She cooed over it softly. Then she pressed it all over. When her tiny fingers reached its throat, she felt a hard lump. She opened the bird's mouth and found a big round manzanita seed sticking in its throat. The seed was just big enough to choke a little bird.

"Oh-h-h, if I had been here in time you wouldn't have died!" thought Wahss. "I could have taken the seed out of your throat." She carried the little bird to the herbwoman. The herbwoman told her to toss it away in a bush.

But Wahss didn't want to do that. So her mother let her make a little fire from the oak punk in her olla and burn up the pretty bird in the real Indian way. She wrapped the ashes in a sycamore leaf because she had no little olla in which to put them, and she buried the leaf in the soft earth.

"Oh, if you only could have told me, little bird!" thought Wahss. She looked about for something

[1] kī ō′tē.

[152]

to put on the grave — something that she knew the little bird had liked. She could find only one tiny brown feather which had not burned.

"I guess you liked your feather pretty well," said little Wahss. "You couldn't fly in the air without your feather." So saying, she stuck the feather over the grave. Then she ran after her mother.

The herbwoman stopped on the top of the hill and looked all around her. Live oaks grew freely here. Mixed with the oaks were the basket bushes. Their leaves looked almost exactly like the leaves of the poison oak. They glowed like rabbits' ears with the sun shining through them.

The herbwoman sniffed and sniffed. "There are better bushes in the next clearing," she said.

Baby Wahss sniffed and sniffed. Her nose was

[153]

very little and stubby, but she could smell something strange. It smelled like a skunk.

"Is it a skunk?" she asked her mother.

"It is not a skunk," said her mother. "It is the basket bush."

"It does not smell nice," said Wahss.

"It smells nice to a basket-maker," said her mother. "How could I carry my herbs if I did not have a basket?"

The herbwoman began to snip off the branches of the basket bush in the next clearing. These branches had a very strong odor, especially when she snipped them. They bent easily.

Then the herbwoman sat down in a comfortable spot and began pulling off the outside bark of the branches. It was the twig inside the brown bark that she wanted for her basket — the clean, white twig. She peeled off the bark with her thumbnail. "Some of the women can't do that,' she said to herself. "They soak it off. But I am an herbwoman. An herbwoman knows many secrets."

Baby Wahss was having a secret all to herself during this time. She was gathering some basket twigs behind her mother's back. "I am going to surprise her when I get home," she thought. She stuffed the basket brush into the little net that one of the old sisters in the wild-rose patch had made for her.

## Wahss Surprises Her Mother

When the herbwoman started for home, little Wahss kept well behind her. Her mother didn't know anything about the surprise.

On the way home the herbwoman passed the huge nest of a pack rat, or wood rat. The nest was built on the ground. It looked like an Indian hut that had fallen down in the east wind. It was built of sticks.

"Aha!" thought the herbwoman. "Now here is something I like. I haven't eaten a wood rat for a long time."

She put down her basket twigs and sat down by the nest. She picked up a strong stick that lay beside her. "I'll whack him when he comes out," she said.

Wahss stopped where she was, away from her mother. She didn't want her mother to see the surprise she had for her. And she didn't want her footsteps to make the earth shake. Even a child's footstep would be felt by a rat. And then he wouldn't come out of his house.

Her mother sat as quietly as a rock rests on the ground. She didn't move a hair. She held up the stick in her hand. Wahss sat as still as a little rock.

While they were both waiting for the rat, Wahss noticed for the first time that she was sitting under an elder bush. The elderberries looked like tiny frosted green apples. She wondered if she could pull down a branch without scaring the rat.

A twig hung over her head. Just as she raised her arm — *whack!* and her mother's stick came to earth. It happened so quickly that the rat didn't ever know he had been struck.

"Elderberries and rat! Elderberries and rat!" cried Wahss, not forgetting in her excitement to gather a bundle of elderberry branches. She was very happy thinking about the good supper they would have that night.

Her mother spent the rest of the day preparing basket twigs for the three old sisters in the wild-rose patch; for one was blind, one had rheumatism in her hands, and the other, — we will just whisper it, — the other was lazy. But it would have been too bad to make two of the sisters go without a basket because of the third.

The roasted wood rat and the cool elderberries were just as good as Wahss had expected, and soon after supper she fell asleep. She slept beside the warm ashes of the fire. Her mother always fixed the fire so that not one spark flew out.

In the middle of the night Wahss woke up with a low wail. "O-o-o-o-o!" She felt as if red ants were crawling all over her. Or perhaps a nettle was pricking her. Or perhaps — "O-o-o-o-o!" she wailed, like a coyote.

Her mother rose from beside her on the earth floor and looked her all over in the soft firelight.

## Wahss Surprises Her Mother

"You have been poisoned with poison oak," she said. "Have you been touching it?"

"O-o-o-o-o!" wailed Wahss.

Her mother poked a stick into the fire, lighted it, and looked about the hut. She found the net that the old sister in the wild-rose patch had made for Wahss. The net was stuffed with poison oak.

"I thought it was basket brush," sobbed Wahss.

The herbwoman said clearly to her daughter, her words falling slowly: "Poison oak looks very much like the squawbush, the basket bush. It grows in the same places too, which makes it harder to tell one from the other. But the leaves are larger. There is always one sure way that you can tell them apart. Sniff them! The basket bush smells like a skunk. But don't get your face too close when you sniff."

"O-o-o-o-o!" wailed Wahss. "I shall always sniff before I pick."

"It is well," said the herbwoman. "It is better to think once than to cure twice."

So saying, she took a piece of baked salt, mixed it with water, and made a wash for her little daughter. The wash cooled all the little red flames in Wahss's skin. She slept again. But she was not cured of the poison oak for over a week.

# ‣ 5 ‣

# *The March to the Piñon Country*

As THE years went by, little Wahss grew wise in all the secrets of the forest. She learned the good of every plant. She learned that goodness lies sometimes in the leaves, sometimes in the seeds, sometimes in the roots. She learned that some medicines are cooked and that some are not. She learned that there was much more to learn. That meant that she was really learning. When one thinks there is no more to learn, he knows next to nothing.

The herbwoman never stopped learning, either. She was just like her father, the medicine man. She was always stewing herbs in the olla, and she was always discovering new herbs. Indians from a long way off came to her to be cured.

She was interested in different things to eat too. She was often trying out recipes that she had made up herself. She liked many nuts of the forest, and especially she liked the piñon nuts. She always joined the other Indians when they marched away on their great piñon journey in the fall of the year.

## The March to the Piñon Country

The Indians were talking about the journey. It was time to go. The women gathered together in little groups and chatted about the things that they were going to take. The men made many new arrows and twisted new strings for their bows.

The herbwoman prepared herself with everything that she needed for the trip. She wore her basket cap and her net. She filled her net with many things — an olla for roasting the piñon nuts, a little water jar, a winnowing-basket, a large seed basket, and a few other things.

Wahss was old enough now to walk with the rest. She was a grown-up girl. She packed her net very carefully. She didn't pack it with poison oak now! She carried a basket, a deerskin package of wild-oat seeds, and some lizardtail roots for sore throat.

"If I do not need them, someone else will," she thought to herself.

The tribe started at early dawn. The little village was nearly deserted. Only a few Indians stayed at home. The thatched houses were almost empty except for heavy things like stone mortars, pestles, and metates. All the other things were tucked away in the nets of the women. The men walked ahead, with their bows and arrows in their hands.

The herbwoman did not walk with the rest of the tribe. She kept by herself, and Wahss followed

her. Her mother was always searching for some new herb that she had not found before.

She couldn't stop in the middle of the trail to gather herbs, because then all the other Indians would have to stop. She wandered a little to one side. All interesting people cannot keep exactly in the trail. "Aha!" she cried, as she saw a new leaf or flower.

Many tribes started from their villages for the great piñon feast. They flowed, like many little rivers, into one big stream. They came from mountaintops and lowlands and middle mesas[1] in between. A mesa is a high, flat meadow with steep, sloping sides. As the people moved along they lighted fires so that others could see where they were and how fast they were going.

Little Wahss could see smoke rising from mountaintop to mountaintop. She could see streams of Indians walking down the mountains. It made a strange feeling in her heart to see so many rising smokes and to think of so many people. All different kinds of people too!

Because here came medicine men and herbwomen; olla-makers and basket-makers; singers and flute-players; hunters, dancers, and old men and women who knew the secrets of the witches.

Here came fathers and mothers, and children of all ages and sizes. Each one that came was thinking a different thought. Little Wahss could feel many thoughts in the air.

One tribe passed her on the trail. She was walking near the path behind her mother. Their long hair fell to their knees. The women were painted in red designs, and the men were painted in white. The women wore aprons of otter skin instead of willow bark, and around their necks they wore strings of shells.

[1] mā′sas.

"They have come from the ocean," said little Wahss to herself when she saw the shells.

Another tribe passed her on the trail. It was a small tribe. One young Indian danced along in front of his people. He shook a rattle made of the shell of a turtle.

"Have you been dancing and singing all the way?" asked Wahss as he passed her.

"I have been dancing and singing all the way," he answered. He gave courage to his tired people.

"And what have you been singing?" asked little Wahss.

"I have been singing about the mountain sheep," said he. "I have been singing about the horned toad and the desert lizard."

"His tribe has come from the desert," thought little Wahss.

And still another tribe passed her on the trail. These Indians were coated with mud. The mud clung to their legs, which had strong muscles.

"They have been wading through mountain streams," said Wahss to herself. "They have been walking in muddy trails."

[ 163 ]

## Secrets of the Trail

Wahss begged her mother to hurry. She wanted to see the Indians all gathered together in one place. But her mother would not be hurried. She was finding new herbs all the time. She dug and dug with her digging stick.

Wahss forgot about the other Indians when she found a new flower herself. She wondered if the flower were good for the chest or the throat or the head. She asked her mother.

"It is good for one thing," said the herbwoman. "When the Indian is hungry for something sweet, he sucks the juice out of this flower." The flower was red. It was the hummingbird's trumpet. Somebody else besides the Indian liked the sweet juice in the flower.

Wahss sucked the juice of the flower, and it was sweet. She wished that she had time to gather many flowers and squeeze the juice into a little olla. She wondered how long it would take.

But now her little bare feet were getting tired, and her back ached from the weight of her pack. Just as she was wondering how much farther they should go that day all the tribes met together on a great mesa.

This mesa was dotted over with the ashes of old campfires. The Indians had planned to camp here for the night to break their long march to the piñon country.

## The March to the Piñon Country

Wahss had never seen so many Indians together before. Cahuilla [1] Indians from the desert, short and fat. Yuma Indians, tall and strong like the Yuma cousin. The Yuma cousin had left her Kum-mee-i cousins and had joined her own people.

She didn't look so strange with the Yumas as she did with the Kum-mee-is. The Yuma women were tattooed on the forehead and the chin, and the Yuma men wore their long hair in dozens of tiny twists.

Little Wahss heard strange languages that she had never heard before. She heard words that were almost like her own but were just a little different.

She saw many little girls of her own age. They looked at her with great round eyes, but they did not speak. She wondered if she should know them better soon. She saw babies and babies and babies.

The Indians began to make camp. The women slipped off their basket caps and nets. The men stacked their bows and arrows against bushes of sage. Each one knew where he had put his bow and arrows.

The Indians began to light their fires. The herb-woman lighted her own little fire with the punk she carried. She boiled some of the wild oats for supper. These wild oats were smaller than the oats the Spaniards brought to the land.

[1] kah wē'yah.

[ 165 ]

## Secrets of the Trail

Little Wahss ate the mush and then curled up against her comfortable mother and fell asleep. The fire kept them both warm.

The Indians were very quiet that night. Their legs were too tired for dancing. They wanted to save their strength for the long journey the next day.

# ▸ 6 ◂

## *Bathing in the Mud*

---

EARLY IN the morning the Indians started forth to
the piñon groves. The women put on their loaded
carrying-nets again, and the men picked up their
bows and arrows. They all began to climb a hill
that stretched before them.

Wahss and her mother walked behind the others.

"Go slower, and you will go faster," said her
mother. "We mustn't miss a single thing."

Wahss noticed that her mother's net grew fuller
and fuller. The nets of the other Indians were not
so full.

"Why don't you dig the roots on the way back?"
asked little Wahss.

"Do you ever see anything so good the second
time as the first time?" asked the herbwoman.

"No, I never do," said little Wahss.

"When we go back we shall see fresh things,"
said her mother. "But they will not be these things.
Our eyes will pick out the things that we have not
seen before."

Noontime came. The sun was hot. It warmed

the Indians a little too much. The sweat poured
down their cheeks. Their breath came quickly.
They walked a little faster, as if they were hurrying
toward some pleasant thing.

"I feel that everyone is thinking of something,"
said Wahss.

"They are," answered the herbwoman. "I am
thinking of something myself."

"And so am I," said Wahss. She wanted to
seem important, too, but she couldn't think of anything except how uncomfortable and hot she felt.
She wondered what everybody was thinking. She
knew that they all had the same thought.

Pretty soon Wahss and her mother reached the
top of the hill. They looked about them. The air
was cool and windy up there. It felt like a cool
hand on their hot cheeks. The breeze blew through
their black hair.

All the lines of Indians were meeting at one
point. It was as if many streams were joining in
the ocean. The tribes from the coast, the tribes
from the mountains, the tribes from the desert —
all were meeting together. Smoke rose from fires
as far back as the eye could see. Indians were
still coming.

Wahss ran ahead of the herbwoman. "We are
going down there," she said, "among all the
people."

## Bathing in the Mud

The herbwoman called her back. "Follow me. Do not lead. I am wiser than you. Who knows what may be in the path?" Wahss stepped behind her mother, and carefully they made their way to the edge of the Indian throngs.

It seemed as if all the animals in the world had come to a water hole to drink. But instead of wild animals they were brown Indians on two feet.

The men stacked their bows and arrows against queer bushes that Wahss had never seen before. The women hung their baby cradles on a curious tree that stood alone in the middle of the mesa. Naked children stepped forward.

Little Wahss clung to her mother's side and held tightly to her willow skirt with her strong little fingers. The child had never seen such a place as this.

She had seen water holes. She had seen running water in the creek. She had seen water pools in the hollows of a rock. She had seen drops of shining water on leaves. But she had never seen the ocean.

"Is this the ocean?" she asked her mother.

"No," said her mother. "This is not the ocean."

"Then what is it?"

"See what it is. Feel what it is," said the herbwoman.

Wahss looked with wide-open eyes. The good old earth seemed to have changed to a sleeping animal with a black skin. The animal was breathing. Wahss knelt down and picked up a wad of dripping black mud. Then she stuck her bare brown toes into the mud beside her. It was soft and warm.

"The earth looks like an olla full of boiling mud," said Wahss.

"That is just what it is," said the herbwoman. "It is boiling, breathing mud down below. These are mud springs. But they are not too hot to burn us."

Wahss watched her mother. The herbwoman tested the mud with her toe, and then she walked right into it! Wahss wanted to scream, but her mother had taught her to keep her feelings to herself. Her mother sank down and down until the mud stopped at her waist. Then she stayed right there.

She twisted her hair out of the way. She threw the mud all over her chest and arms. She seemed very happy sitting in the mud. She wore a strange smile that Wahss had never seen before. She seemed to forget about Wahss.

All the other Indians were sitting in the mud pools and smiling. Some of the young boys were throwing mud at one another. The children were playing like squirrels.

Wahss stepped carefully into the mud. Oh-h-h!

## Bathing in the Mud

Something was pulling her down. She felt herself going, going, going! She could not hang onto anything. There was nothing to hang onto except one little blade of grass. She seized the grass, and it broke off in her hand. Then she screamed!

Her mother turned quickly. She still wore that happy smile. "You are perfectly safe," she said. "You can go no farther than your chest. Have no fear. You should have waited for me to tell you everything, but now you have learned for yourself.

"It is a kind mud. You can only go just so far. Then a hand holds you up. It is the same hand that pulls you down." And the herbwoman splashed in the mud like a turtle.

Great tears gathered in the child's eyes. But she trusted her mother. She soon found that she could go no farther down than her chest. She even tried to push her way farther down, but she bobbed up like a cork. She became braver every minute.

"It is kind mud! It is kind mud! The same hand that pulls you down holds you up!" She felt cozy and comfortable in the mud. She began to smile just the way her mother was smiling.

"This mud is good medicine," said the herb-woman. "It cures rheumatism."

"I haven't any rheumatism," said little Wahss.

"You have no rheumatism now," said the herb-woman. "But you may have rheumatism some day. It is well to learn today what we need to know tomorrow."

Wahss smiled to herself. She was really very glad to know that it was good for rheumatism. She was storing up in her mind all the cures for sick people. She wanted to be just like her mother some day.

The Indians played in the mud all through the early afternoon. Then they rinsed themselves in a clear pool, rested a while, and started once more for the piñon groves.

# › 7 ‹

# *Nighttime in the Forest*

---

IT WAS early evening when they reached the heart
of the grove. The air was sweet with pine needles.
The needles were smaller than Wahss had thought
they would be. The piñon trees were straight and
well-formed.

Wahss thought she had never been in a pleasanter
camp. It seemed as if each tree were her friend.
Good trees that could give nuts to eat and branches
to burn! Good trees that could give shelter and
shade and comfort!

Her mother selected a place for their camp under
one of these beautiful trees. Many yellow piñon
cones shone like gold near the top of this tree.

"The piñons on this tree are ripe," said the
herbwoman.

She kindled a fire out of the dry piñon branches.
Wahss gathered little sticks and helped to feed the
fire. Then she rested beside the fire because she
was very tired. As she spread out her hands at
each side of her she felt something soft and sticky
on them.

[ 173 ]

## Secrets of the Trail

"What is this funny stuff sticking to my hands?" she asked.

"It is pitch," replied her mother. "The piñon trees are covered with pitch."

Wahss rubbed her hands on her knees, and her knees became sticky, too. "I am covered with this sticky stuff!" she cried, a little frightened. "It is all over my body."

"Rub earth on your hands and knees," said her mother wisely. "The earth will stop the pitch from sticking."

Wahss dusted the sticky places with dry earth and cleaned off all the pitch. "Earth is clean, isn't it?" she asked her mother.

"Earth is clean sometimes," answered her mother. "It is like medicine — good for some things and not good for other things."

"It is good now," said little Wahss.

Her mother set an olla over the fire, poured acorn meal into it, and covered the meal with water. She had brought a sack of the meal in her net. Soon a nice mush was bubbling.

"Our supper will soon be ready," she said. "Did you bring some crushed stones of holly berries? We will put them in our mush."

Wahss felt very proud to help with the supper. She opened her deerskin bag and poured a handful of powdered stones into the mush.

## Nighttime in the Forest

"I like the mush spiced with holly-berry stones," said her mother, smacking her lips.

"So do I," said Wahss.

The mush bubbled and boiled.

"Fix our bed for the night before it gets too dark," said the herbwoman.

Wahss looked about her. She had never seen a place like this before. The ground was covered with dry black cones that hurt very much when one lay on them. She looked over toward her mother to ask some questions, but her mother was busy.

So Wahss took a long stick and scraped away the pine cones until the ground was clear. Then she gathered many soft long grasses. She coiled these grasses into a cozy round bed. "We can snuggle together on this bed," she said.

"Hun!" said her mother. "The fire will keep us

warm tonight. It is not very cold. Tomorrow the brother of the Yuma cousin will make a shelter over our heads."

The acorn mush was ready. The herbwoman dipped it out with an oakwood spoon into two clay bowls. "Be very careful of your bowl," she said to Wahss. "We have brought only two."

Wahss held the bowl very nicely. She didn't want to break it. If she broke her bowl she would have to put her mush on a piece of pine bark until her mother made another bowl. But perhaps the right kind of clay couldn't be found in the piñon country. Then she wouldn't have another bowl until she reached home.

She curled her first and second fingers into a little spoon and ate her mush. It was very good mush. The herbwoman always soaked out all the bitterness from the acorns. One of the old sisters in the wild-rose patch said that she liked a little bitterness in the mush. "Some people like funny things!" thought Wahss.

The herbwoman and Wahss cozily ate their supper together. They looked around the forest. Many campfires sparkled in the openings. Circles of Indians sat around them. Their backs, as they bent over their supper, looked golden in the firelight. Some of them had twisted up their hair. Paint marks decorated their skins.

## Nighttime in the Forest

Their voices were as soft and deep as the wind in the treetops, and they sat as quietly as tree trunks. Those who were moving at all moved like shadows. They seemed to belong to the forest.

The thin moon was curled like half the rim of a winnowing-basket. There were as many stars as cherries on a cherry bush. The *mi-h'tut*,[1] the "backbone of the sky," which some people call the Milky Way, was in its place as ever.

At the edge of the brush a coyote wailed like a frightened child. Perhaps he was afraid of the strange new lights in the forest.

Wahss fell asleep over her mush bowl. She didn't know that her mother gently took her bowl away and laid it upside down by the tree trunk. She didn't know how nearly she had broken it, for, had it fallen, it might have hit a stone.

The herbwoman snuggled down beside Wahss and covered the child's little body with her long, warm hair. Soon the piñon country was as quiet as if it were not filled with Indians of many tribes and from faraway places.

[1] mī h'tŭt'.

# ▸ 8 ◂

# *Wahss Spoils the Water Hole*

---

WHEN WAHSS awoke she saw her mother kneeling by the fire, roasting seeds of the wild sage. The camp lay in half darkness. Dawn had not come. Wahss shook herself and ran over to her mother because she felt cold without the blanket of hair.

"My water jar is empty," said her mother. "Go to the water hole and fill it."

Wahss didn't know which way to go to the water hole. But she didn't like to bother her mother by asking too many questions. Her mother had taught her this: Think first; ask last.

Wahss set a ring of fiber on her head and set the water jar on the ring. The water jar was rather small. Some of the women had brought their big water jars with them.

As little Wahss turned away from the campfire she saw other Indians with water jars on their heads. They were following a certain trail. Some of them were coming and some of them were going. She joined the ones that were going.

She could just make out the trail in the twilight

## Wahss Spoils the Water Hole

of the morning. It was a tiny trail. It led this way
and that way among the forest trees, and then it
ran down into a sandy creek bed.

"This creek is dry," thought Wahss. "But
perhaps there is a deep hole somewhere that has
caught the rain water."

The little girl had guessed right. Under an old
piñon tree whose roots spread out of the ground
a stream had rushed quickly one day. It had
whirled and whirled about until it had made a

deep hole. In this hole some of the hurrying water had rested. This was the water hole.

The women walked single file along the bed of the creek until they came to this water hole. They carefully stepped down to the edge of the pool. The mud was slippery. One woman knelt down, leaned on her hand, and drank deeply. The mark of her hand stayed in the mud.

Wahss looked closely for other marks. She saw the fresh tracks of a little fawn. She saw the neat tracks of a wildcat. How she loved the little round toes of the cat! She saw the tracks of the coyote who had howled in the early evening, and she saw the handlike tracks of a raccoon.

"I love water holes," thought Wahss. "We cannot live without water. I guess all the little animals of the forest love water holes, too."

She waited until the women had filled their jars; then she started to fill her little jar. As she stepped nearer the edge her foot slipped on the mud and she almost fell into the hole.

"Phut!" cried one of the women sharply. "Do you not see what you are doing? You are spoiling our water hole with mud!"

It was so indeed! The beautiful, clear water hole was dark and muddy. It was spoiled! Wahss crept back and sat on one of the roots of the tree. She felt like crying; but she didn't cry, because she was an Indian. Sometimes Indians cried, but not often. This was not one of the times.

She was very glad that she had waited for the women to fill their jars before she spoiled the water hole.

She stayed by the pool until the water had cleared a little; then she threw some brush over the mud and knelt on the brush so that she should not slip. She skimmed the clear water off the top.

On the way back she met some more women with water jars on their heads. "They will know I spoiled the hole," she thought sadly. "I will never do it again."

Her mother poured some water into a bowl and lifted the bowl to her lips. "This is good water," she said. "It is rain water."

"I think it is good water, too," said Wahss, "when it hasn't been spoiled."

Her mother didn't know what she was talking about.

They ate their breakfast happily. Everything tasted so good in this strange land!

"Why didn't we take a bath before we ate our breakfast?" asked Wahss, as she dried her lips with the back of her hand.

"Because there was so much to do this morning," said her mother. "We can take our bath in the

early afternoon. Tomorrow morning you can take
your bath at dawn."

The forest began to grow light. Wahss could see
all the Indians that she knew and some that she
didn't know. She could see her old grandfather, the
medicine man, sitting with the men of her tribe.

Her old grandmother and the three old sisters in
the wild-rose patch had stayed home. She could see
the Yuma cousin sitting with her Yuma people.

The women were getting ready for their day's
work. They were putting on their basket caps, so
that the pitch wouldn't stick to their hair. They
were lining their nets with leaves.

The herbwoman put on her basket cap and gave
Wahss a long stick.

"Come," she said.

Wahss followed her mother. The herbwoman
walked straight along until she came to a tree with
golden cones all over the top.

"Why don't we pick the nuts on our own tree?"
asked Wahss.

"They have all been picked," said her mother.
"I could see none on the ground. Other Indians
have been here before us."

Wahss began picking up the nuts under the tree.
She put them in a little basket which she carried.

"You will never get through picking if you pick
that way," said her mother. "We only pick them

[ 182 ]

that way when we are tired of climbing trees. That is the way a coyote gathers nuts — one by one. Only he eats them as he gathers them. Are you a coyote?"

"I am not a coyote," said Wahss, "but I drink out of the same water hole." She remembered the tracks in the sand.

As she finished speaking she looked up, and her mother was not there! Why, she was there just a second before! Where could she be? Where — where was her mother?

Then Wahss heard a curious noise in the tree and, looking up saw her mother almost at the top! She was climbing like a squirrel! Some of the branches were so old that they broke off. But her mother always found new branches.

"Watch!" called her mother. "I am going to throw down some cones." Before Wahss had time to move, the herbwoman threw down a cone and hit her right on top of the head.

"I'm glad it wasn't a sticky green cone," said Wahss to herself. But it was a little sticky, just the same. She moved away after that. Her mother threw a great many cones into one pile.

"Beat out the seeds with your stick," she called to Wahss.

The little girl started beating the cones, but some of them were a little sticky and stuck to the branch.

"They're sticking to the branch," cried Wahss. "What shall I do?"

"What did you do to your sticky hands?" called her mother from her perch in the tree. "Throw some dust on them. Then they won't stick."

Wahss did as her mother said, and then she could beat out the seeds much better. When she had beaten out all the seeds, she gathered them into the basket that she carried and poured them into her little leaf-lined net. The little seeds, the shape of date seeds, were warm brown in color.

All the morning long the herbwoman climbed trees and threw down cones. She always threw them down in piles, so that the seeds could be beaten out together. One young Indian woman in another tree threw them down any way at all. It took her a long time to run around and beat out seeds. It was her first visit to the piñon country, and she didn't work like an old-timer.

"It is not hard when you know how," thought Wahss. She felt very proud of her wise mother.

When the sun was hot, the herbwoman said: "Now we will take our bath. We will gather no more nuts until it is cool again."

Wahss was very glad to stop beating out the nuts. Her little back ached. "I can straighten out in the water," she said.

Wahss had bathed in many pools. She wondered

what this pool would be like. She followed her
mother up some steep rocks. The rocks were so
rough that she did not slip. One rock was almost
flat on the top. In this rock were several smooth
little hollows.

They were the little hollows that Indian women
had made by grinding seeds. They were not the
deep acorn holes.

"I should like to live in the piñon country," thought little Wahss. "There is everything here that a woman would need."

The herbwoman stopped climbing the rocks. She stood before a cave. The roof of the cave was stone. The walls of the cave were stone. The floor of the cave was — water! It looked like a stone swimming tank.

"The sun only gets in here very early in the morning," said the herbwoman; "so the water is very cold." There was just one doorway to the stone room. This doorway faced the east.

Wahss stuck her foot into the water. It was as cold as snow in the evening. Then she slipped in all over. One end of the pool was very deep. Her mother followed her. They sat up to their necks in water.

"This is a nice place," said Wahss. "Tomorrow I will come up here when the sun is shining through the doorway."

Wahss and her mother cooled off in the rain-water pool. They washed their hair too. Then they sat on the rocks in the sunshine and dried and brushed their hair. The herbwoman had made new brushes for the trip. They were neat little brushes of yucca fiber.

When their hair was smooth and shining, the herbwoman laughed.

## Wahss Spoils the Water Hole

"Why are you laughing?" asked Wahss. Her mother did not often laugh so suddenly. Her laugh usually came slowly and left slowly.

"I am laughing because we washed our hair," replied her mother. "We forgot ourselves because we felt so cool in the water. We should not wash our hair until the last day of camp. It will only get covered again and again with pitch."

Wahss smiled wisely. "If we have nice hair we shall take better care of it," she said. "We shall stay out of the pitch."

"If we can," laughed her mother.

The two playmates walked down the huge rock steps to the piñon trees. Soon they had forgotten their fun. They were too busy gathering piñon nuts. Not until suppertime did they rest.

# An Old Woman Hides Her Nuts

AT DAWN the next morning little Wahss ran up the rocks and bathed in the stone room. The early sun shone in through the doorway. She played happily in the sunny water.

When she was walking down the trail to her camp, after climbing down the rocks, she met an old Indian man digging a pit with a sharp stick.

"Why are you digging a pit?" she asked.

The old man pointed to a pile of sticky green piñon cones.

"I am going to put these cones in it," he answered. "This is the way to cook unripe nuts."

Wahss sat down on the ground and watched him. He made a very deep round pit. He smoothed it out until it was clean and nice. Then he kindled a fire in it.

When the fire had died down, he scraped away the ashes, threw dust on the sticky cones, and laid them neatly in the pit. Then he covered them with earth and scraped the ground smooth. One would hardly know that anything had been buried there.

## An Old Woman Hides Her Nuts

"How long will it take to roast them?" asked Wahss as the old man smoothed the earth.

"Not very long," said the old man. "While you are eating your breakfast they will roast."

Wahss had forgotten all about her breakfast. She ran back to her piñon tree. Her mother had already left the camp for her nut-gathering. She had covered the fire with ashes.

By the side of the fire, wrapped in a leaf, was a quail. Wahss guessed that it was a present to her mother from the brother of the Yuma cousin. She guessed that her mother had left it for her. She roasted it over the flame.

After her breakfast of quail she ran back to the old man. He was just beginning to uncover the cones. Wahss wondered what they would look like. They had been roasted a light brown. Wahss picked one out of the pile.

Ouch! It was so hot that she dropped it.

"I will wait until it is cool," she said to the old man.

"If you wait until it is cool, it will close up again and you cannot get the seeds out. You must get them out while it is hot. Work quickly. See!"

The old man took a hot cone, quickly opened it with his fingers, and showed Wahss many brown seeds lying in pairs.

Wahss picked up a cone and, after dropping it twice because it was so hot, opened it and found the seeds. She discovered that she could jerk the cone open swiftly and the seeds would fly out. That was better than digging them out with her fingernails.

"Now these are already roasted," said the old man. "We shall not have to parch them over the fire."

"Why don't you always prepare them this way?" asked Wahss.

"Because they do not taste so well as when they

are ripe," he said. "I am going to look for the ripe ones now." So saying, he covered the cones with dust to keep them hot and walked away.

While Wahss stood quietly watching him go, an old woman passed her. The old woman carried a deerskin sack on her shoulder. She was walking on a trail which led up a little hill through a growth of juniper bushes.

Wahss secretly followed the old woman. She followed her up the hill, over a pile of rocks, and into a cave. She peeked into the cave and saw the old Indian dump her sackful of piñon nuts into a tall olla which stood on a ledge of rock.

Before the old woman had time to turn around in the cave Wahss had slipped away. She ran quickly to her mother, who was just starting to climb a tree.

"An old woman is hiding her piñon nuts in a cave!" she cried.

"Hush! hush!" said her mother. "Hush! What you know, do not tell. What you tell, do not know. Never follow anybody again. Should you like to have anybody follow you? Keep to your own trail!"

Wahss felt very much ashamed. But she couldn't help thinking about the old woman. Why was she hiding her nuts in a cave so far from home? What good were some hidden nuts going to do her?

Just then she saw the old woman returning, carrying an empty sack.

"Who is that old woman?" asked Wahss, turning to a young Indian man who was sitting under a tree fastening feathers in a new arrow.

"That is Liss," answered the Indian.

"Where does she live?"

"She lives here," said the young Indian. He pointed to a little hut at the edge of the brush.

Wahss didn't say anything, but she guessed now that the old woman had a reason for storing nuts in her own back yard.

All during the day Wahss helped her mother to gather the piñon seeds. Toward noon the sun was so hot that she sat under the low branches of the tree. Many brown nuts were scattered among the tiny needle-like leaves.

"We will pick up these nuts right here," said her mother, taking off her basket cap and sitting down beside her little daughter. "This is a slow way, but it is better than no way at all." She had done enough tree-climbing for a while.

Patiently they gathered the nuts, one by one, one by one. Wahss had gathered almost a basketful when her mother suddenly noticed what she was doing.

"You are picking up some old nuts with the new," she said. "Do you see these dark-brown nuts? They are good. Do you see these pale nuts? They are not good. They are too old." She pressed a pale nut between her fingers, and out popped the dust.

"The brown nut feels heavier than the light-colored one," said the herbwoman. "And there is another sure way to tell." She gathered up a handful of nuts, held them in the palm of her hand, and blew lightly upon them. About half of them blew away.

"Those that stay in the palm are good," she said. "They are too heavy to blow away."

"I think all that blowing takes too long," said Wahss.

"You will not need to do that after a while," replied her mother. "You will pick up the good ones without half looking. You will learn to do it quickly."

It took a long time to pick up the little nuts one by one when they were scattered thinly all over the ground. It was easier to gather them when they were in a pile, after they had been beaten out by a stick.

Wahss ate every other nut that she picked up, even though they were not roasted. It was fun to do this, because she could never eat acorn meats until the bitterness had been taken out.

She happened to move around to the side of the

tree where the sun could creep under the boughs. She picked up some more nuts. She tasted one. It was hot! It tasted exactly as though it had been roasted.

"These nuts have been roasted!" she cried to her mother.

"They have been roasted by the sun," said her mother. "There are more ways of cooking than cooking by fire."

"I think cooking is interesting," said Wahss. "When I am grown up I am going to learn many secrets about it."

"Do not wait until you are grown up," said her mother.

They picked nuts until suppertime. While they were making their supper fire her mother said: "We will toast some of our nuts now. I can hardly wait to eat them. Sometimes I don't eat another thing but nuts when I am in the piñon country."

Wahss carried a basketful of nuts to the fire. The herbwoman poured them into a cooking-olla and set the olla on the three rocks grouped around the little fire. She stirred the nuts constantly with her oak spoon.

"You do it," she said to little Wahss.

Wahss took the stick and stirred the nuts. The smoke of the fire blew straight into her eyes, but she was used to smoke.

## An Old Woman Hides Her Nuts

"You are not stirring quickly enough," said the herbwoman. "Quickly, or they will burn!"

Wahss stirred them as fast as she could. *Pop!* sang one. *Pop!* sang another. *Pop!*

"They are jumping out of the olla!" cried little Wahss. "Soon I shall have none left."

"They are moist," said her mother. "That is why they pop." She clapped a shallow clay dish over them to keep them in their little hot house. Then she held the small cooking-olla with a leaf and shook it quickly. "Now I guess they are done," she said.

Wahss uncovered the olla. There were the little nuts, toasted to a deep, cheerful brown. She let them cool off a bit; then she picked up one, cracked it with her teeth, and ate it, spitting out the thin brown little shell. The meat inside was the color of cream.

"Hun!" she cried. "This is the best nut that I have ever tasted. It is not like the acorn. It is already sweet."

"Yes, it is already sweet," said her mother. "We have nothing to do but toast the nuts, and they are ready to eat. But we can make dry meal out of them if we wish. Then we can eat a handful at one time. Some people like them best that way."

Little Wahss wanted to make the meal that very moment.

"Shall we cook it then? Like acorn meal?" she asked.

"Of course not," said her mother. "These nuts have already been cooked. There are more ways of cooking than boiling or roasting. Toasting is one of the best ways of cooking."

"Oh!" cried Wahss. She would be happy when she learned the wisdom of her mother.

"How do we make the meal?" asked the little girl.

Her mother said nothing. Instead, she walked to a tree near them, put her hand into a hiding place under the roots, and dragged out a heavy metate and a round rubbing stone. She poured some nuts upon the metate and ground them up with her stone.

"Now hand me my winnowing-basket," she said to Wahss.

## An Old Woman Hides Her Nuts

The herbwoman scraped the meal into her winnowing-basket and winnowed away the brown husks. When the meal was clean she tasted it.

"Hun!" she said. "It is good. It is sweet and rich and good. Who could wish for better food?"

"No one," said little Wahss, as she tasted the meal. "It is good. But I think I like the nuts better when they are not ground into meal."

"So do I," said her mother, smiling. "We shall not grind our nuts. Let the old people grind theirs. Then they will not have to crack shells with the teeth they haven't got."

Wahss felt very happy. She had learned four ways of preparing the piñon nuts. One way was to beat the seeds out of the cones and toast them. Another way was to roast green cones in a pit and open them when they were hot. The Indians could come early to the piñon country and do this before the nuts were ripe. Another way was to pick the seeds off the ground and toast them. And still another way was to grind the toasted seeds into meal.

"I shouldn't be surprised if there were still other ways," thought Wahss. "Some day I will try to find out for myself. I like to find out things for myself best. I should like to be an herbwoman like my mother. I should like to spend my days discovering medicines and good food for people."

### Secrets of the Trail

"This has been a long day," said the herbwoman, as she lay down in a warm spot in the little shelter. The brother of the Yuma cousin had made them a tiny hut. "A long day, but a happy one."

"All days are happy to me," said little Wahss, as she snuggled under the long hair of her mother.

# ‣ 10 ‧

## *Tub-sho-kwitl, the Piñon Game*

---

THE FOREST was echoing with the laughter of the Indians when little Wahss awoke. Young women chatted gaily together in groups, old women squatted on the earth in a wide ring, and children darted among the trees. Young men and boys and a few old men were gathering together in a circle, their long hair whirling in the breeze. Their bodies were brightly painted.

"Something seems to be turning over in the hearts of the young men this morning," said little Wahss to her mother.

"You are right," said her mother. "They are going to play *tub-sho-kwitl*,[1] the 'piñon game.' We will wait a little while and watch them. I see that the other women are not yet going to work."

The piñon game! Wahss had heard of this game many times, but she had never seen it. She climbed up a tree so that she could have a better view. Other children scrambled up beside her and hugged the branches like little bears.

[1] tŭb shō kwĭtl'.

The Indian game of dart and ring! The game that is played only in the piñon country! The game that is played with only the materials that grow there! The piñon game!

An Indian with a feather tied to his hair was building a fire at the foot of a slanting rock. Little Indian boys were gathering pitch from the piñon trees. The pitch shone in the sun like golden beads.

When the fire had heated the rock, the Indian brushed away the burning twigs and dug a little basin at the foot of it.

Then the young Indians ran to the rock with their golden pitch and laid the pitch on top of it. With a burning torch they set the pitch on fire.

## Tub-sho-kwitl, the Piñon Game

Now the pitch began to melt and slowly run down in thick rolls. The Indian with the feather in his hair stuck a stiff yucca leaf into the rolling pitch and wrapped the pitch around it. What the leaf did not catch fell into the basin.

As the golden pitch ran down the rock the Indians all sang together:

### Tub-sho-kwitl [1]

**AN INDIAN GAME AND CEREMONY**

*Sung over and over by the Indian at his fire to help make the pitch run in good rolls. Originally sung softly in a man's falsetto voice.*

Hŭn-yah-yah'    Tĭl - tōl - ah'    mĭl - mĭl - ah'
Pitch          running        down

Kah-pī - yah  pī-yah   Kah-pī - yah  pī - yah
in good, good  rolls,  in good, good  rolls.

Their happy voices rang gaily through the forest. The chickadee took up the thread of the song and sang "Good rolls, good rolls!" in his chickadee language. The brown towhee in the dark piñon branches echoed "Good rolls!" in his towhee language. All the forest seemed to be singing.

[1] Sung by Santos Lopez, a Kum-mee-i Indian. Transcribed by Harold Kimball, principal of Cabrillo School, Point Loma, San Diego, California.

## Secrets of the Trail

"Wouldn't the pitch run down if they didn't sing the song?" asked little Wahss of an older girl who clung on a bough beside her.

"Oh, never! never!" cried the older girl.

"Why didn't they melt the pitch in an olla?" asked Wahss.

"And get the olla so stuck up that it's no good for cooking?" scolded her tree companion.

Now, while another Indian began turning the yucca leaf for him, the young Indian with the feather in his hair brought forth a young hawk that he had killed with his bow and arrow. He pulled the feathers out of the wings and tail. All the young men rushed over to him, and each grabbed a feather.

The little fellows couldn't run and grab so fast. They didn't have any feathers. So they dashed around until they found some barley beards — tall grasses that look like feathers.

Then each man and boy sharpened a stick on a rock and stuck the pointed end of the stick into the hollow quill of a feather. The little fellows tied their grasses to their sticks with fiber.

Then each one dipped the other end of the stick into the pitch around the yucca leaf. They spat on their hands and rolled the pitch into a nice round ball. Then they rolled the ball in the dust, so that it wouldn't stick to everything. The ball was as big as a hawk's egg.

## Tub-sho-kwitl, the Piñon Game

Now each had a dart about ten inches in length with a long feather at one end and a ball of pitch at the other.

But the darts alone were not enough for playing the piñon game. So they all made rings out of twigs. The rings were about three inches across.

The Indian with the feather made the best ring. He was a coast Indian. He wore a necklace of shells.

All the Indian men and boys lined up in a row. The coast Indian tossed his ring away from him, and it landed on the ground. One by one the Indians threw their darts at the ring. The brother of the Yuma cousin threw his dart nearest the ring, so he became the ring man. He was going to hold the ring!

He kept one of the darts for himself, and the other Indians picked up the darts that had been thrown.

Now the brother of the Yuma cousin stood apart from his fellows and held the ring in his hand. He was very tall, with long hair twisted into tiny rolls. His face was tattooed in dark blue. He had a circle on his forehead and stripes on his chin. His broad chest was painted in huge circles and dots of white. His arms were longer than the arms of the Kum-mee-i. His body shone with sweat.

Wahss thought him very handsome indeed.

One by one the other Indians threw their darts
into the air. The feathered shaft looked like a
flying bird. The golden ball of pitch shone in the
sun.

As the Yuma stood there boldly, with his feet far
apart, he caught every dart in his ring. Sometimes
the hard ball of pitch struck him on the knuckles,
but he didn't move a muscle.

As he caught the dart he let the ring and dart
fall to the ground. If the dart fell out of the ring
as the ring was falling, he could not keep his place
as ring man.

## Tub-sho-kwitl, the Piñon Game

"I don't see how he can catch every one," whispered little Wahss to her tree companion.

"Hush! hush! Now you have given him bad luck. He is losing!" Just at that second a dart fell out of the Yuma's ring as the ring was falling. The Yuma brother was no longer the ring man.

He gathered up all the darts at his feet. He kept one dart and started to throw the others back to the Indians. Suddenly he raised his arm as if he were going to throw them in their faces, and then — he tossed them over his shoulder!

The young men and the old men almost fell over one another in their speed to pick them up. The little boys dashed on the heels of the young men. What a scramble!

One little fellow got pushed out of the way. He couldn't find even one dart! He lay on the ground under a pine tree and began to sob. And as he sobbed he felt something sticky touch his cheek. He was lying right on a dart! It was feathered with barley grass. It was his own dart! He grabbed it and rushed back to play.

The Yuma brother tossed the ring away from him. The Indians again threw their darts toward the ring as it lay on the ground. Another Indian won the place of the ring man. And so the game went on.

The women could wait no longer. They had

work to do. They took up their baskets and nets and started for the thickest part of the grove. Wahss climbed down the tree and ran over to her camp to fetch her little basket.

"Oh, I wish I were a boy instead of a girl," she thought. "Boys have such fun!"

# ‣ 11 ‧

# *The Cherry Bush*

---

THE HERBWOMAN and Wahss stayed in the piñon country only one more day. The herbwoman wished to start home before the others. She wished to gather herbs all the way. She would meet the other Indians at home.

"This is our last day here," said the herbwoman to Wahss.

"What are we going to do?" asked Wahss.

"We are going to hunt for every good herb of the forest. Everything one could wish is here."

They covered the breakfast fire with ashes, put on their basket caps and nets, and started up a little trail which ran toward the north.

"Keep your eyes open," said the herbwoman, "and anything that is here will be seen by you. We must not leave the piñon country until we have taken all there is to take."

They had not walked far when Wahss spied a juniper bush dotted with berries.

"These berries look like good things of the forest," she said. "I have never seen them before."

## Secrets of the Trail

"*Hah!*" (Yes!) said her mother. "They are good things indeed. Pick all you can."

Many of the berries had fallen to the ground. Wahss found that it was easier to sit on the ground and pick them up than to pull them off the bush. Besides, there were only a few left on the bush.

"Gather the biggest ones," said her mother. "This is not the only bush of these berries."

"Do you toast these too?" asked Wahss.

"No, no," said her mother. "They are too thick-skinned to toast. We will boil them in the olla when we get home again. They are blue now, but they will turn brown while they are cooking."

Wahss thought that these berries were very interesting. Almost everything in the piñon country was new to her.

After they had gathered a small sackful between them, the herbwoman started slowly on, looking always about her. Soon she began to sniff the air.

"There is much basket grass here," she said, "but we have plenty of that at home. We will not load ourselves with things that are not necessary."

"This basket brush is a little different," said Wahss, looking at it carefully. "The leaf seems a little thicker."

"It is thicker," said her mother. "What plant would not grow thicker in a snowy land?"

# The Cherry Bush

"What is a snowy land?" asked Wahss, her eyes wide open with wonder.

"A snowy land is a land covered with snow," answered her mother. "Snow is a soft covering like a rabbitskin blanket, but it is white instead of gray. It falls through the air as lightly as floating rabbit fur. But it is not warm like rabbit fur."

"Why does it fall?" asked Wahss.

"It falls so that it will melt and give us water in the valley," said the herbwoman.

"When does it come?"

"It comes in the winter. In the winter the pine trees will be white with snow. All the Indians that live here will visit our warm valleys or the desert until it is gone."

Wahss tried to picture the pine trees covered with bits of rabbitskin blanket, except that the rabbitskin blanket in her mind was white rabbitskin.

"Shall I see it some day?" she asked.

"You will see it from far off, maybe," said the herbwoman. "You will see it on a mountaintop. But you will not see it close to us if I am with you." She laughed softly.

"I do not like snow in this skirt," she said. "I have heard about some Indians far away who wear deerskin clothes and moccasins. They are not afraid of the snow, because they have clothing like that of a deer."

## Secrets of the Trail

Wahss couldn't possibly imagine any other Indians besides her own Indians and the Yuma Indians and neighboring tribes. Once she had seen a Ko-ko-pah [1] Indian, but he did not wear deerskin. He ran away when he saw her Indians. The Yumas and the Kum-mee-is, her Indians, were friendly, because a long time ago they had all belonged to the same family. But the Ko-ko-pahs were enemies.

"*E-yi!*" suddenly cried her mother. "Here is a cactus plant with ripe fruit." The fruit was a dark rose color.

"Shall we take the fruit home?" asked Wahss.

"No, no," said her mother. "We have plenty at home, and it would be hard to take, anyway. We will eat some now." They ate cactus fruit until their lips were crimson.

"The cactus seeds are good to eat, too," said the herbwoman. "We will toast them some day when we have nothing better. We will mix them with water. They make a nice thick drink."

They passed many good things that grew at home. They passed yucca stalks, which are so good when roasted. They passed the pointed leaves of the mescal.

"It is not the season for roasting the roots of the mescal," said the herbwoman. "Besides, we can get plenty of mescal whenever we go to the desert."

[1] kō kō pah'.

[ 210 ]

# The Cherry Bush

As they turned a bend in the trail they suddenly came upon a bush brilliant with red cherries. It was the holly-leaved cherry bush.

"Oh-h-h!" cried Wahss. "Are those berries good to eat?"

The herbwoman didn't say a word. She had waited a whole year for this sight. She pulled off some cherries as fast as she could and popped them into her mouth. Then she took off her basket cap and filled it to the brim with the cherries. She poured the cherries into her net, which she had lined with leaves. She filled the basket again and again.

Wahss didn't talk, either. She ate one cherry; then another; then another. She had never eaten anything that was so good. She too filled her little net with cherries.

The forest seemed built around this cherry bush. It was as if the cherry bush were a fire in the center of it. Even the birds seemed happier near the cherry bush.

The bright blue jays whirled over it. The towhees, those neat fellows dressed in orange and black, gathered around it and warmed their coattails at the fire. How unlike were these towhees to their brothers, the brown towhees! But sweetest of all were the chickadees, those cheery little elves of the forest.

They swayed on the tip ends of the cherry bush and called, "Chickadee-dee-dee! chickadee-dee-dee!"

"I have learned something," said Wahss, as she chewed the cherries.

"And what is that?" asked her mother.

"These cherries are not boiled or roasted or toasted in the sun. They are eaten raw!"

They had come to the end of the wandering trail.

# The Cherry Bush

Now the herbwoman made her own trail. She walked around the edge of fallen trees. She circled big rocks and bushes. Little Wahss followed her mother, sometimes changing the trail a little to suit herself.

"I like to make my own trail," thought little Wahss. The herbwoman noticed that Wahss didn't follow step for step, although she followed in a general way.

"She will not need me always," thought her mother. "She picks her own trail. It is good."

As they were walking quietly along they heard voices. Coming upon a wide clearing, they saw a party of young Indian men carrying curved wooden rabbit sticks.

*Whiz-z-z!* One of the rabbit sticks was whirling through the air! It hit a rabbit in the neck; but the rabbit didn't even know that it had been struck, it had all happened so quickly. Soon the air was alive with whirling sticks.

"We had better not try to cross this clearing," said the herbwoman. "The young men will think we are two jack rabbits and will aim at us. It is time to go back to camp, anyway."

They passed an elder bush on the homeward trail. Only a few pale berries stayed on the bush. The berries hung at the far end of one branch. A brown towhee was finishing them up.

"He is eating the last berries on the tree," said the herbwoman. "It is no matter. The elder bush grows at home."

"Are the blossoms good to eat?" asked Wahss. She had never noticed her mother picking them.

"They are very good for fever," answered her mother, "when they are stewed. I always carry some with me. I have some now. And they make a nice broth for tiny babies. We Indians give our babies elder broth before we give them milk. That is why Indian babies are strong."

Wahss wondered what the white people would

say about that. She had seen only a few white people, but they seemed to be traveling on another trail from the Indians.

When Wahss and her mother were drawing near their camp, they passed a little group of Kum-mee-is. One of the old women of this group was melting pitch in a tiny olla.

"Why is she doing that?" Wahss asked her mother.

"She has rheumatism," answered the herbwoman. "Melted pitch is very good for that. She brings the little olla with her just for melting pitch."

"I hope she will not rub the pitch on before it cools a little," said Wahss, as she watched the hot pitch bubble in the olla.

"She has been using pitch medicine for twenty autumns," said the herbwoman. "I guess she knows how to put it on by this time."

"I hope that I may know all the medicines some day," said Wahss.

"You will know all the Indian medicines if you learn one every day," said the herbwoman. "But how can you ever know all the medicines of the white people?"

"I shall not need to know the medicines of the white people," said Wahss, as they reached their camp.

The herbwoman said nothing. She kept silent while they ate their supper.

# · 12 ·

# *Why We Argue Today: A Story*

---

IT WAS evening. All the Indians were gathering round their fires. It was the last evening that Wahss and the herbwoman were planning to stay in the piñon country. How long would it be before they came this way again?

"Your grandfather, the medicine man, is going to tell a story tonight," said the herbwoman to Wahss. "Let us hear what he has to say."

Wahss and her mother joined the Indians at the fire. Many groups of Indians were circling other fires. Other medicine men were telling stories, too.

Wahss sat between her mother and the Yuma cousin. All the rest of the women crowded around them. The men sat on the other side of the fire. In the middle of them squatted the medicine man. The shell in his nose flashed in the firelight.

The darkness closed around the Indians like thick black walls. The smoke from the fire smelled of pine and sage. The fire whispered in a cozy voice. It was trying to tell a story of its own.

The medicine man said: "I will tell you the

# Why We Argue Today: A Story

story of Per-ah-ahk[1] and Per-ah-hahn.[2] It is an old, old story that my grandfather told me when I was a little boy. I have never forgotten it, and I never want you to forget it. I want you to tell your grandchildren when I am gone."

So saying, he held the palms of his hands before the blaze and repeated the story of "Per-ah-ahk and Per-ah-hahn," or "Why We Argue Today."[3]

In the days of long ago there lived a young woman named Sin-yah-how.[4] She was the mother of twin babies. Per-ah-ahk was the name of the older twin, and Per-ah-hahn the name of the younger.

[1] per ah ahk'.     [2] per ah hahn'.
[3] From a legend told by Santos Lopez, a Kum-mee-i Indian.
[4] sĭn yah how'.

## Secrets of the Trail

Early every morning the mother went forth into the forest to gather seeds. She left the babies in her little thatched hut, safely wrapped up on their cradleboards.

One evening when she returned with her basket full of seeds she heard a thin little voice singing a song to her babies. She looked all around the hut, but she could see nothing.

At last she lifted up the stone metate lying on the earth floor, and under the metate she saw a singing cricket. She let the metate drop back again, and it dropped right on the cricket's legs and broke them! That is the reason why the cricket hops today.

Every morning after Sin-yah-how left the hut to gather seeds in the forest, the babies crept out of their cradleboards. They tiptoed forth to the mesa to shoot quail. They carried tiny bows and arrows with them.

But they always crept back into their cradleboards before their mother returned. They left quail in the corner of the hut.

Every night Sin-yah-how saw the birds and wondered who had brought them to her hut. Who could be shooting quail? And every night the babies cried and cried. They wanted their mother to eat the birds.

One night Sin-yah-how cooked one quail and

pretended to eat it. The babies didn't cry any more. Now their mother knew why they had cried.

The next evening, when Sin-yah-how was returning from the forest, she saw baby tracks in the sandy trail.

"Aha!" she thought. She said nothing; but early the next morning, on her way to the forest, she turned herself into a tree stump. She sat by the trail where she had seen the baby tracks.

After a while the two babies freed themselves from their cradles, took their bows and arrows, and started off to hunt. They saw the tree stump by the trail.

"We have never seen this stump before," said Per-ah-ahk, the older brother.

"No, we never have," said Per-ah-hahn. "Let's shoot it." They pulled back their bowstrings.

Then their mother cried out: "It's your mother! It's Sin-yah-how!" She turned herself into their mother again and started up the trail.

After that day the babies never went back to their cradles. They were big boys now. They began to think of going farther and farther. They decided to hunt for a nest of young eagles for arrow feathers for their arrows.

"Go," said Sin-yah-how, "but be sure and have no argument over the older of the two young birds, or you'll start rainy weather."

The boys slept all that night, and the next morning they ate nothing because they were going on this far journey. They could walk faster when they were light. They walked and walked until they came to the rock where the eagles lived. The rock looked very slippery.

"I'll try to climb up the rock," said Per-ah-ahk, the older brother. The younger brother sat down at the foot of the rock. The older brother tried to climb up, but the rock was too slippery.

"Now I'll try it," said the younger brother.

"No, no; you can't do it," said the older brother. They began to argue. The weather grew foggy.

"All right; try it," said the older brother.

Per-ah-hahn changed himself into a lizard and crawled up the rock. Rattlesnakes and scorpions were sitting around the nest of the eagles.

The younger brother reached into the north and pulled some sand out of the air. He sprinkled the sand on the animals. They all melted away in a jiffy.

Then he took the two young eagles that were sitting in the nest, cradled them in his net, and crawled down the rock. When he reached the ground he changed back to his old self.

As soon as he looked at the two eagles the older brother said: "You take the younger bird. I'll take the older one." The older one of the two baby eagles had larger, prettier feathers.

## Why We Argue Today: A Story

They argued about the older bird. The weather grew more foggy. It began to rain. They argued some more. Hail came and wind. The older brother picked the younger bird out of the net.

"Come on!" said the younger brother, going ahead. He carried the older bird. He held his chest away up as he walked along. The older brother lagged behind with the younger bird.

It rained hard all the way home. The two birds died on the way. The boys buried them in the earth and broke their bows and arrows over the grave. Sadly and slowly they walked to their hut.

As soon as Sin-yah-how saw her two boys she knew that something had happened. But she said nothing.

Early the next morning she faced the north, waved her skirt, sang some magic words and brought the two birds to life. They flew to her hut and lit on the ground.

Sin-yah-how called her sons, who were sleeping in the hut. She told them that the birds were alive.

"We will see," said they, running to the little doorway.

They saw the two birds resting on the ground. They each rushed over to the older bird and picked it up. They argued and argued.

"Let it alone!" cried Sin-yah-how. "I'll fix everything."

[ 221 ]

The young eagles wouldn't eat. So she went into the forest and found a nest of young crows. She turned the crows loose and fed them. When the eagles saw the crows eating, they began to eat, too.

Sin-yah-how kept the eagles tame until they were full grown. Then she killed them. She sent the boys into the marshes for arrow shafts. Then, when the little fellows were sleeping at night, she made two bows and a bunch of arrows.

The next morning, while Per-ah-ahk and Per-ah-hahn were playing outside the hut, Sin-yah-how brought out a fine bow and some arrows. The boys argued and argued over them.

The mother laughed. She went back into the hut and brought out another set of bow and arrows. It was exactly like the first. So each boy had a nice bow and arrows, with the arrows feathered in eagle feathers.

And they became great hunters forever afterward.

And this is the end of the story of Per-ah-ahk and Per-ah-hahn. But the people in the world are still arguing, just because those two argued long ago!

The camp was quiet. Everybody was listening for one more word. But not one more word came.

Then the herbwoman said to Wahss: "We will go to bed now. We must get up early in the morning."

## Why We Argue Today: A Story

"I don't want to go to bed," whined Wahss. "I want to hear another story."

"Hush!" said the herbwoman. "Are you going to begin arguing, too, and start rainy weather? Come!" And they left the fire and cuddled up together in their little shelter, Wahss wrapped in her mother's long hair.

# ▸ 13 ◂

## *The Camp of the White People*

THE HERBWOMAN and Wahss took an early bath in
the stone bowl, washed their hair, and left the camp
at dawn. They passed the Yuma cousin on the trail.
She carried a water jar on her head.

"Are you going back with your own people?"
asked the herbwoman.

"Yes," said the Yuma cousin. "I am going back
where the river is wide and long and the mesquite
beans are sweet."

"It is well," said the herbwoman. "Each one
should stay in the place she likes best. I am going
home, too, but I am going to take a new trail."

"Do not get lost," said the Yuma cousin.

"Do not fear. I have always found my way,"
answered the herbwoman.

She branched off from the old trail and took a
new trail to her home.

"Few have traveled over this trail," she said to
Wahss, "but you and I are trail-makers. We do
not like trails that have been ground down by
everybody's feet."

## The Camp of the White People

Many times they walked where no one had ever stepped; for the trail was completely grown over in places, and they kept losing it and finding it again. But soon the trail looked as if many footprints had pressed upon it.

"Someone besides Indians has been walking here," said the herbwoman, staring at the earth. "These people wear shoes. They have been walking up and down the trail to this little spring." Sure enough, a clear little spring flowed out of a rock at the end of the beaten path of the trail.

"Are they white people?" asked Wahss, her heart in her mouth.

"Who else?" replied the herbwoman.

Wahss shrank back. "Let's go to camp again and start out on the other trail," she said. "I do not like white people. They are so cold looking, and they have loud, ugly voices."

"Not all of them," said the herbwoman. "I knew a white woman once who was very kind. Her voice was like the running water in the creek. Come."

The herbwoman started bravely forward, but Wahss hung back.

"Come! come!" cried her mother. "You will have to meet the white people face to face some day. You will meet them many times. It is good to begin now."

[225]

## Secrets of the Trail

They walked slowly along, one behind the other. Soon the herbwoman lifted her head and began to sniff.

"I smell the white people's camp," she said. "They are near."

Wahss caught her mother's skirt. "Do not let us go past," she begged. "Let us go back."

"Trail-makers never go back," said her mother. "Have you forgotten that your mother is an herb-woman; that your grandfather is the medicine man; that your old, old great-grandmother has discovered almost all the secrets in the woods? Let us go and find out the secrets of the white people. We shall need them if we ever live in their world."

The herbwoman marched along, and Wahss followed bravely, ashamed of her fear.

They had not gone very far when they came in sight of the white people's camp. They saw a homemade tent, a covered wagon, and colored clothes hanging on the branches of trees. They saw a white man carrying a bucket of water and a white woman gathering wood.

When the white people saw the Indians coming, they stopped working and began to talk together in low tones.

Wahss and her mother stood perfectly still, like a deer and a fawn who have been surprised. "Their

## The Camp of the White People

voices are not loud or ugly," thought Wahss to herself. "Perhaps they are kind too."

Just then the white woman came slowly toward them. She beckoned to the herbwoman and said something to her that they couldn't understand.

The herbwoman whispered to Wahss: "She is anxious about something. I must go to her." She knew when a person was troubled.

She left Wahss standing under a pine tree and

walked bravely toward the white woman. The woman smiled at her and beckoned to her to come into the tent.

When Wahss saw her mother go behind the flap of the tent door, she felt as if a cloud had been wrapped around her. She could not move she was so afraid. The man stepped into the tent, too.

It seemed many moons before her mother came out again. When she left the white people, she smiled at them and they smiled at her. They seemed happier than they had been before.

"Let us hurry to the next spring," said the herbwoman to Wahss. "It is just below here. I am thirsty. The white people are lucky. They have a spring on each side of them. But they do not know about this spring. They know only about the one we have just passed."

Wahss asked her mother no questions about her visit in the tent. She knew that she would tell her everything when she was ready.

The herbwoman climbed up some rocks at the side of the trail and lifted up a large flat stone that lay on one of the rocks. She uncovered a deep, narrow well of water!

"Oh-h-h!" cried Wahss. She had never in all her life seen a spring like this.

"Quiet!" whispered her mother. "We must keep some things hidden from the white people. This spring must always be saved for the Indians, so that we can be sure of water when we need it."

The herbwoman knelt by the spring and took her own little brown bowl out of her net. The bowl was stained dark with something wet. She filled the bowl and sipped the water slowly.

"A sick boy lay in that little cloth hut," said she. "He was hot with a bad fever. His cheeks were as red as holly berries. His father and mother didn't know what to do. Their medicines were all used up."

She kept on sipping the water in her bowl. Then she said proudly: "I am an herbwoman, even for the white people. I stewed him some dried elder blossoms that I was carrying in my net. He drank out of this bowl. That is why it was wet. Now he will live." She filled the bowl again for Wahss.

The little girl and her mother rested on the rock for a long time. The weather grew foggy. Then rain fell.

"I guess Per-ah-ahk and Per-ah-hahn are still arguing," laughed Wahss. Her mother did not laugh.

Now it was pouring.

"We cannot go on," said the herbwoman. "I know a cave near here. We will stay there until the rain is over."

## Secrets of the Trail

They climbed farther up the rocks until they came to a little cave. It was like a little rock room with stone shelves in it. They took off their basket caps and nets and put them on the shelves.

The herbwoman kindled a fire on the earth floor and set the cooking-olla on three stones. It was very chilly in the cave. There was no way to shut out the cold wind.

"We will make the best of it," said the herbwoman.

It rained for several days. Wahss and her mother were half frozen all the time. The weather had changed. It smelled of snow.

"Perhaps I shall see the snow at last," said Wahss.

"I hope not," shivered her mother.

One night Wahss woke up and heard her mother tossing on her bed of leaves.

"I am cold and then I am hot," said the herbwoman in a strange, weak voice; "I am hot and then I am cold."

"That is funny," thought Wahss to herself. "That is just the way I feel, too."

Then her mother said, "When dawn comes go into the forest and gather some more elder blossoms."

"It is too late for elder blossoms," said Wahss. "It is not springtime." She wondered how her mother could forget.

## The Camp of the White People

"Then get me some other good medicine," said her mother, tossing on the floor of the cave.

At the earliest light of dawn Wahss started down the mountain toward the camp of the white people.

"Perhaps there are some elder blossoms left in the little cloth hut," she thought. "Perhaps my mother didn't stew them all. She always carried enough elder-blossom medicine for the whole tribe."

But she had another reason also for going to the camp of the white people. She remembered their kind faces and their low voices, and she knew that she and her mother needed friends.

# ▸ 14 ◂

# *The New Trail*

---

WAHSS WOKE up in a strange room. The walls were not thatched with brush. They were smooth walls. The room was light, not dark like the room of the little hut at home. And it was high, so high! She thought it almost touched the clouds.

She was lying on something high too. She was used to sleeping on the warm, smooth earth. She had a white cloth under her and a white cloth over her. She knew cloth when she saw it, because she had seen the white people wearing it.

Wahss had been very sick. When she ran down the mountain to fetch the elder blossoms, she felt dizzy and faint. As she reached the camp of the white people she almost fainted at the door of the tent. She just had time to tell them by signs that her mother was sick in the mountain cave and then she didn't know anything at all.

The white people took care of her. They didn't tell her for a long time that her mother had died. Then they told her as well as they could, by using signs.

## The New Trail

Both Wahss and her mother had caught the sickness of the little boy by drinking out of the same bowl from which he had sipped. The herbwoman had saved his life but had lost her own. She had never learned anything about germs.

When Wahss didn't get any better, the white people took her to a hospital in a mining town. It was only a little hospital, but it seemed huge to Wahss. When the white people felt quite sure that Wahss would be given good care, they journeyed on to other places.

Tired little Wahss had fallen asleep in the covered wagon on the long, long ride to the hospital, and she did not know when the nurse tucked her into bed.

Now a tall white woman rustled toward her bed. She wore white clothes. She looked like a floating white cloud to little Wahss. The white woman carried something in her hand.

It was not a basket. It was flat with a little rim around it. There was a shiny tall thing standing on it. Wahss could see right through this thing! It seemed to be filled with a white soup. But the soup was not steaming like rabbit soup.

"Drink your milk!" said the nurse, passing her the tray. Wahss didn't understand what she said, but she understood what she meant.

She took the strange shiny glass (for that's what

it was) between her fingers and sipped the white soup. Oof! It was cold and horrid. She spat it out!

"Oh!" cried the nurse. "You mustn't do that!" She took the glass away from her. Wahss had never learned any of the manners of white people. If she didn't like anything, she always spat it out.

She looked all around her. Other little girls rested in other beds. (She learned later that she was lying in a bed.) The other little girls were white and coffee-colored and pale yellow.

She supposed that the coffee-colored ones were Mexicans and that the pale-yellow ones were Japanese. They were very pretty. Her mother had told her about these two races. In one bed was a little white girl whose bright golden braids were tied with blue ribbon.

Wahss felt of her own hair. It was mussed. It was ragged. It was filled with bits of seeds and thorns and twigs.

If she were at home or in camp she would have brushed her hair with her hairbrush. She didn't know where the white lady, the nurse, had put her hairbrush. And she didn't know how to ask.

If she had a handful of yucca fiber she could make a little brush. She looked all around the strange room. She didn't see any fiber at all. She didn't see a single thing in this room that she could use for anything.

## The New Trail

The nurse washed and dried her hair and brought her a little white comb. Wahss didn't know what it was. She hid it under her pillow.

Pretty soon she saw a little girl combing her hair. Then she knew how to use a comb. But it wasn't nearly so nice as the brush!

Then the nurse gave her a bath. Wahss couldn't help laughing to herself. She had always taken her bath in running water. Or in deep, quiet pools. Or in the mud! She had never had a bath brought to her!

When suppertime came Wahss looked very carefully at all the things on her tray. She smelled everything.

There was a yellow mush that looked like the

spilled eggs of a blue jay. There was a thin bowl of stewed greens that looked like the medicine clover that her mother used to gather. There was a dish of something that looked like frogs' eggs. How could Wahss know that it was tapioca pudding?

She didn't know that there was a first and last to any meal. She had never heard of a dessert. She had never seen a knife and fork and spoon. Her knife and fork and spoon were her own little brown fingers.

So she curled her little fingers around the frogs' eggs and whipped the pearly balls into her mouth.

"Oh! oh!" cried the nurse, who was hurrying by at that moment. "No, no, no!"

A kind-looking doctor was standing behind the nurse. He was known in the hospital as Doctor Ben. He was watching little Wahss with the kindest eyes she had ever seen.

"A little Indian!" he said to the nurse. "She is just like a little wild rabbit. While she is here we shall teach her many things. But think of all the things she can teach us!" Wahss didn't understand what he said, but she knew that Doctor Ben was a good friend.

After Wahss had stayed in the hospital a few months (for she had been very, very sick) she knew many strange things. The nurse had taught her to drink milk and to eat the food of the white people, how to comb her hair nicely, how to use a knife and fork and spoon, and how to brush her teeth.

Wahss had the nicest, prettiest teeth of any of the children, but now that she was eating the food of the white people she would need the brush of the white people too.

Doctor Ben used to sit by her bed a little while every morning and give her lessons in English. She learned many words from the other children too. Soon she could speak a little English and could understand very much. She even learned Mexican and Japanese words also.

One morning the doctor said: "You are almost well. Soon it will be time for you to leave the hospital. Do you want to go?"

"No," said Wahss. "You good to me. I no place to go. My mother dead. My grandfather, the medicine man, and my old, old great-grandmother, all living with other peoples. They no need me."

"Ah!" said the doctor, speaking slowly. "Now I will tell you a short story. Not so very long ago the Indian medicine man and the Indian doctors could always cure their people. The herbwoman could always cure her people.

"The sickness the Indians had was only Indian sickness. The wise ones of the tribe knew a cure for every sickness.

*Secrets of the Trail*

"But now it is different. The Indians are beginning to catch the same sickness that the white people have. They have caught their new sickness from the white people, just as you and your mother caught your sickness from the little white boy.

"Your mother could cure the little white boy with elder blossoms, but she couldn't cure you or herself with elder blossoms. The white sickness is much more dangerous for the Indians than it is for white people, because the Indians are not used to it."

Doctor Ben looked straight into the dark eyes of little Wahss.

"Do you want to learn how to cure your own people?" he asked. "Do you want to learn to be a nurse and go among your own people and teach them our secrets? Do you want to be a new herb-woman?"

Wahss looked straight back into his eyes.

"Yes, I do," she said. "My mother die because she not know what to do. But how can I learn," she asked, "if I go away?"

Doctor Ben took her little brown hand in his.

"You will not go away," he said. "You will stay right here, and I will teach you. As soon as you are strong enough you will help me to take care of all these children.

"When you have learned the white people's

secrets, we shall go together among the Indians until you can go alone. When they are very sick you will bring them to the hospital."

"How long it take to learn white secrets?" asked Wahss.

"It may take ten years before you learn them well enough to teach them," he said. "But every day will be a busy one for you until then. I am going to bring the sick Indians here right now, and you can translate the Indian words into English words for me while you are learning to be a nurse."

"Ten years!" exclaimed Wahss.

The doctor looked at her for a long time.

"Ten years," he repeated. "Have you patience?" He watched her closely.

Wahss lifted her head proudly. Her eyes flashed. "I am an Indian," she said. "Indians have patience — all time."

Doctor Ben smiled happily. "All the great people in the world have patience," he said. "Work without patience is like a river without water."

And from that very day Wahss started to learn the secrets of the white people. But she never forgot the secrets that the herbwoman had taught her. It was only one step from the old trail to the new.

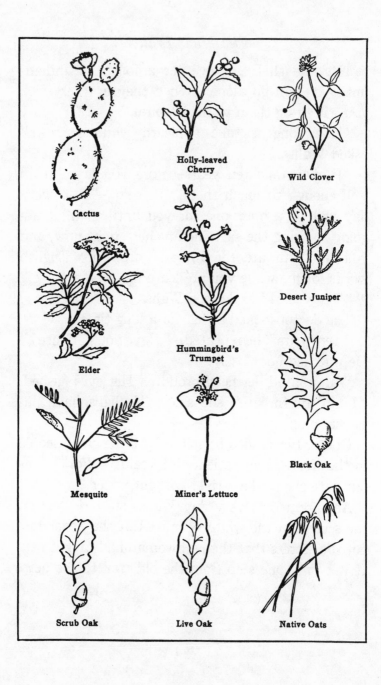

Cactus

Holly-leaved Cherry

Wild Clover

Elder

Hummingbird's Trumpet

Desert Juniper

Mesquite

Miner's Lettuce

Black Oak

Scrub Oak

Live Oak

Native Oats

*Herbs that the Herbwoman Used for Food and Medicine and Her Recipes for Preparing Them*

---

## FOOD

**Cactus** (*tuna*), or **prickly pear** (*Opuntia Lindheimeri* Engelmann). Eat the fruit raw. Parch the seeds, grind, and mix with water.

**Cherry, holly-leaved** (*Prunus ilicifolia* Walpers). Eat the fruit raw. Crush the stones in a mortar, soak out the bitterness, and boil into mush.

**Clover, wild** (*Trifolium*). Boil like other greens. Good food and good medicine too.

**Elder** (*Sambucus glauca* Nuttall). Eat the fruit raw.

**Hummingbird's trumpet,** or **scarlet bugler** (*Penstemon centranthifolius* Bentham). Suck out the sweet juice.

**Juniper, desert** (*Juniperus californicus*). Boil the berries until soft.

**Mesquite** (*Prosopis juliflora* De Candolle). Grind the pods and let the powder harden in molds in the ground. (A recipe borrowed from the Yuma cousin.)

**Miner's lettuce** (*Montia perfoliata* Howell). Eat the leaves when tender or stew like other greens.

**Oak, black** (*Quercus Kelloggii*); **oak, scrub** (*Quercus dumosa*); **oak, live** (*Quereus integrifolia*). Grind the acorns, winnow, soak out the bitterness, and boil into mush. Eat with rabbit. Very good.

**Oats, native.** Boil into mush.

[ 241 ]

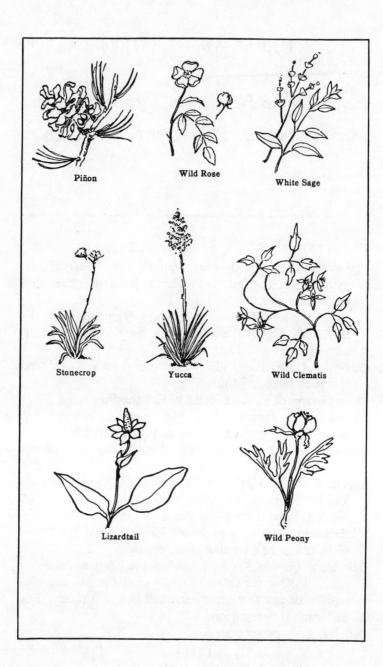

Piñon

Wild Rose

White Sage

Stonecrop

Yucca

Wild Clematis

Lizardtail

Wild Peony

# Herbs and Recipes

**Piñon** (*Pinus quadrifolia*). Parch the nuts. Eat plain, or grind into meal, or roast the nuts in the ground while still in cones (this is done when the cones are green). Very good.

**Rose, wild** (*Rosa californica* Chamisso and Schlechtendal). Eat the rose hips (fruit) raw.

**Sage, white** (*Audibertia polystachya* Bentham). Boil the seeds into mush. Eat the tender tips of the stems.

**Stonecrop, or baby fingers** (*Dudleya edulis*). Eat the tender tips of the leaves.

**Yucca, or our Lord's candle** (*Yucca Whipplei* Torrey). Roast the young stalks in ashes.

## MEDICINES

**Clematis, wild** (*Clematis lasiantha* Nuttall). Stew the blossoms and use as a wash for rheumatism.

**Clover, wild** (*Trifolium*). Boil like other greens. Good medicine and good food too.

**Elder** (*Sambucus glauca* Nuttall). Eat the berries raw. Stew the blossoms into a broth for tiny babies. Brew the broth for fever.

**Lizardtail, or yerba mansa** (*Anemopsis californica* Hooker). Stew the roots into a broth for a gargle to cure sore throat.

**Peony, wild** (*Paeonia Brownii* Douglas). Stew the roots into a broth for stomach-ache.

**Piñon** (*Pinus quadrifolia*). Melt the pitch for rheumatism.

**Sage, white** (*Audibertia polystachya* Bentham). Steam yourself in the burning leaves after unhappiness or sickness of yourself or others.

# › LITTLE DICTIONARY ‹

## *Indian Words*

---

**Ah-wee-ah-pī′pah:** Slanting Rock. The name of a place on Cuyamaca Mountain, southern California.

**hah:** yes.

**Hah-kwah-nĭtl′:** Black Spring. The name of an Indian village.

**Hah-rō′:** Hot Water. The name of an old Indian man in the story.

**hee-waht′:** deer broom.

**how′ka:** hello.

**hŭm-ĭl-kwah-taht′:** an animal that no white man has seen.

**hŭn:** good.

**hŭn′-nah:** good. (The same as *hun.*)

**hŭp-chŭtl′:** arrow straightener.

**Hŭtl-yah-mī-yŭck′:** Moon in the Sky. The name of the little Indian boy in the story.

**Kō-kō-pahs′:** enemies of the herbwoman's tribe.

**Kŭm-mee-īs′:** the name of the Indian tribe to which Wahss and the herbwoman belonged.

**Kwee-mŭck′:** Cloud Behind. The Indian name for Cuyamaca Mountain.

**Kwee-tahk′:** Little Man. The name of the little white boy in the story.

**kw'nī′:** a rush (juncus reed) used for a basket wrapper.

**kwur-kwur′:** "talk-talk."

**k'yū′:** come.

**mee-yĭp′-ah:** listen to me.

## Little Dictionary

Mī-hee-ah-wĭt'-ah: man who knows everything.

mī-h'tŭt': backbone of the sky; the Milky Way.

mow (rhymes with *how*): no.

N'mee' n'wah': Home of the Wildcats.

n'yah'mah: enough.

n'yah-pūn': a basket-strainer.

Ōp-a-chŭck': the name of the Indian woman who adopted Kwee-tahk.

Per-ah-ahk' and Per-ah-hahn': twins in the legend "Why We Argue Today."

Pī-ōn': the name of the Indian man who adopted Kwee-tahk.

sah-wĭl': a winnowing-basket.

shah-wee': acorn mush.

shō-kwĭn': an acorn-storage basket.

Sĭn-yah-how': mother of the twins in the legend "Why We Argue Today."

tŭb-shō-kwĭtl': a game of dart and ring that is played only in piñon land.

Wah kō-pĭ': House of the Poison Oak.

Wahss: the name of the herbwoman's little daughter.

Yŭ'ma: the name of a desert tribe of Indians.